Shrouds

by

Mae Thorn

Cover Art by *Lea Schizas*

The Wild Rose Press, Inc.
PO Box 708
Adams Basin, NY 14410-0708
Visit us at www.thewildrosepress.com

Publishing History
First Edition, 2025
Trade Paperback Print ISBN 978-1-5092-6357-8
Digital ISBN 978-1-5092-6358-5

Published in the United States of America

Dedication

To the weirdos. The outsiders. The graveyard wanderers. The hellhound seekers. The poets and peacemakers. This is for you.

Chapter 1

The fire popped, jostling Laurel Atwell from sleep. The pop preceded a crackle and a voice that was not her father's. Her eyes widened. They were no longer alone.

Her sister, Allie, groaned beside her but didn't wake. Laurel frowned at her as she slid off the bed they shared. The night peered back at her from the window, and she blinked to uncover any source of light. It was long past midnight.

The voice heightened as she neared the door to her parent's room. The bedroom her father refused to use after the death of his wife, Laurel's mother, though Laurel wouldn't claim the bed.

"What?" Her father's voice shook the windowpane.

"I'm sorry. There isn't any more we can do."

"Are you sure it was hers?"

"Quite sure. They neglected to bury this."

Laurel peeked into the parlor to see Reverend Daniel Carr dangling a dove-white slipper from his thumb and forefinger. Her mother was buried with it.

Laurel gasped and clapped a hand over her mouth. Her stomach twisted itself into knots, rising uncomfortably into her chest.

Her father, Micah Atwell, snatched the slipper from the Reverend's grasp and held it up to his eyes. The thin slipper must have given away its identity as her father pelted the shoe into the unlit parlor fireplace.

"Enough." Micah ripped his coat from the rack. "This isn't the first time someone has desecrated the sacred ground."

Reverend Daniel stepped back. "What are you going to do?" The man's hand shook as he tugged his hat back on.

"We need a grave watcher."

"Mr. Atwell, the church can't afford a watcher."

Her father eyed Reverend Daniel up and down. "I don't work at night."

"But when will you sleep?" Reverend Daniel grasped her father's sleeve but he quickly shook him off.

"That's no concern of yours."

"Everyone in Tenwich is a concern of mine." He paused. "If it hadn't been for Mr. Boswell, we would never have found the slipper." The Reverend shook his head.

Laurel must have made a noise as her father's gaze fell on her.

"Laurel, go back to bed."

She advanced into the room, her arms hugging her middle. "Let me help."

A long moment passed where doubt and anger ruled the air. Her father appeared to tick off reasons she shouldn't go in his head. The truth was, he needed her. She had never been one to help with cabinetry, but she knew the graveyard better than anyone in Tenwich. If a blade of grass was disturbed, she would know it.

Her father sighed. "Get changed."

She didn't wait for him to call back his words but hurried into the old room where she kept her clothes. Her previous room when her mother's gowns still

rested in her parent's room as though waiting for her return. This was not the type of resurrection they had in mind.

Laurel chose her outfit blindly. It didn't matter anymore; everything was dyed black. She managed to fetch her bonnet without tripping on Allie's trunk. Her half-boots and gloves slid on like they were as eager to leave as she was.

Her father still spoke to Reverend Daniel as she returned. Their backs faced her. "It doesn't matter; she's past that. She'll have to earn a living somehow."

Laurel's cheeks heated. They were talking about her.

"It isn't proper. She needs a husband."

She pressed her boot into the squeaky floorboards and the men fell silent. Her father gave her a bright smile, but the Reverend cleared his throat and looked away. She decided to pretend she hadn't heard their conversation. After all, it wasn't the first time someone in Tenwich had commented on her failure to wed.

She forced a smile. "I'm ready."

A spark lit her father's pale green eyes. "My dear, you're always ready."

"Even if I wasn't, it wouldn't stop me." Her grin creased her eyes as she repeated the familiar response.

The Reverend tugged his coat closer and lowered his head as he tugged open the front door. Ice seemed to seep through the air in its quest to gain the warmth of the Atwell residence. They hurried out the door before the cold could reach Allie.

Laurel's breath preceded her, and she followed the Reverend to the churchyard. Crusted leaves crushed under her boots. The lantern light cast a dull glow over

their path, but Laurel could make the trip blind if she needed to.

Not the church itself, but the graveyard was like a second home to her. The sacred ground not only held her mother's memory but also held the stories she had grown so fond of. They were the stories of those who had come before her. The whispers of lives forgotten.

Her mother's grave rested with the other Atwells. Her grandparents, great-grandparents, her aunt and uncle, and her mother's babies, who never made it past infancy. They all seemed to huddle together as though the closeness would keep them warm from the autumn chill.

They had yet to erect a stone for her mother, but the fresh earth left no doubt to the location. It appeared as it had during the day. If the body snatcher hadn't neglected to rebury the slipper, nobody would have known the difference.

The Reverend stopped at the head of the grave. "It was as before."

Her father let out a long stream of breath, clouding the space before him. "They are improving."

Laurel bit her lip, holding back her tears. "How can anyone do such a thing? She never hurt anyone."

Her question was met with silence. Grave robbing in Tenwich made little sense. It was a small town too many hours from a hospital or university. What could they want with her, or the other corpses that had disappeared, some of which the townspeople were no doubt unaware of?

Laurel kicked at the fallen leaves and her jaw clenched against the words she wanted to scream. *Why her?*

"Would you like me to say a few words?" the Reverend asked, his voice uncertain.

Micah Atwell's brows pinched together. "Why?" It was the only sign her father would give that he was angry, but his cool never burst. At least, never that Laurel had seen.

Her father smoothed a hand over the pistol at his hip, and she wished he had let her bring her own, but the Reverend didn't need to know about another failure she had as a lady. It wouldn't help for the town to know she was the best shot her father had ever seen.

Since coming of age, she hadn't given it much thought. Now, at twenty-one, she had few options and fewer suitors. Zero suitors. Her mother wouldn't be pleased if she had been herself the past few years.

The tears threatened again at the edge of her vision. She wouldn't do this now. Crying was something she did in private, and though it was only her father and the Reverend, private did not include them. Not even Allie would see her tears.

"What will we do?" Laurel's words drifted from her thoughts to her lips.

The Reverend placed a hand on her shoulder, and when she flinched, he pulled away. "I'm afraid there isn't anything we can do until we catch whoever is doing this."

"Which is exactly what we'll do." Her father straightened and his gaze seemed to take in the expanse of the graveyard.

Laurel's jaw loosened and her hand searched for her pistol, coming up empty. Some parents spent time reading with their offspring. Laurel's father would wander the graveyard with her at night and shoot pistols in the woods during the day. The townspeople wondered why she wasn't married.

"Good luck to you, Mr. Atwell." The Reverend caught Laurel's gaze. "Keep well, Miss Atwell."

They both nodded to the man as he made his way across the yard. Laurel flinched as she walked over darling Mrs. Boswell's grave without an apology or prayer. She snapped her gaze away and found her father watching her.

He folded his arms. "Go on, Laurel."

Her smile dimpled and she rushed over to the sunken earth. It took her seconds to find her pistol and she added a dagger on a moment's notice. She kicked up her skirts as she ran back to join her father, who looked on over the graves, a slight tilt to his mouth.

"Took you long enough."

Laurel panted. "The Reverend was slow leaving."

"When has that ever stopped you?"

She gave a faint laugh. They both knew her mother would never allow her out in the dark to hunt grave robbers. It wasn't something young ladies should do, let alone own a pistol, and while her mother still had sense, Laurel would never have gone against her wishes. Colette Atwell was dead now, and Laurel could make up her own mind.

They didn't speak as they moved to the far side of the graveyard. The edge was overgrown with trees, the roots claiming the bones. Laurel took slow steps, keeping her boots from rustling the leaves. There was something about the silence she didn't want to disturb. The grave robbers were likely long gone, but the air was heavy with watchfulness.

"Father, will they come back?"

He continued without a pause. "Not tonight. Not until we have another corpse, but by then, we'll be ready."

"Why tonight then?"

He grunted. "We're awake."

He didn't say it, but his stiff stance told her enough. Her father was angry. Angrier than she had ever seen him. It was worse than when they had discovered her mother's illness. As before, her father's anger hadn't burst, but now, she could sense it near the surface. It mirrored her own.

The tension wrapped around her muscles, and she did her best to continue their pace. Laurel bit her lip again and swallowed down her sobs. She rubbed her arms, but not against the cold.

The outskirts of the graveyard crept into the lantern light. The farthest of the gravestones rose in front of them, and her father turned to face the perimeter of the yard when Laurel cried out.

At first, she thought she saw a rock covered in moss, but the color was wrong. The surface was smooth as though water had worn away the edges, but it wasn't a stone. She squinted at the object until it came into focus.

A skull covered in hair.

She couldn't look away as the sunken eyes looked back at her. It was too old to be her mother and too new to be in this part of the graveyard. She picked her way through the trees' undergrowth and the view grew clear.

The skull was attached to the rest of the body.

"Oh, God. That's Mrs. Boswell." She recognized the salt and pepper strands sitting like a mop on her head.

"They left her behind."

"She's been dead for weeks. They've been fooling us for that long."

Her father nodded. "Or they dug her up recently."

"No. Her grave isn't fresh. I would have noticed if it was disturbed. Why leave her here?"

"Why take her at all?"

Laurel's chest tightened, but her curiosity latched on. First, Mrs. Boswell and now her mother. Who else rose from the grave? As far as she knew, neither one of them held anything in common.

"Father, this is worse than we thought." It had started with Widow Sanders. Laurel had found the dirt on her grave had been replaced in a sloppy manner. The Reverend and her father had dug up the grave in secret to investigate and found the grave empty.

"Much worse."

"First, the Widow Sanders and then mother. Now, Mrs. Boswell. Why would someone in Tenwich want their bodies? Why go through so much trouble?"

"Whoever is doing this is getting sloppy."

"Sloppiness means we can catch them."

"Are you ready?"

"I'm always ready."

Chapter 2

Despite the previous night's activities, Laurel started her day as she usually did with a fist full of flowers and a black gown. Her mother's grave was empty save for her mother's clothes, but that didn't stop her from delivering flowers to the site.

The lavender crushed in her palm, emitting a scent she associated with home. Her mother would use the potted lavender to freshen the laundry and decorate the table. It was one of those touches she didn't realize she valued until it was gone. Even in her final days, lavender coated the air in their home. Now it was only a ghost that lingered in their hallways.

Sunset colors painted the trees in her path against the pale blue sky. The air held a bite that hinted at future snow. That air was still much like the town, and every crunch beneath her boots seemed to test the peace.

The graveyard sat as it had before the robbers. No hint of their crime disturbed the ground today. The body of Mrs. Boswell was long since reburied. Her father and the Reverend had dealt with the corpse, not wanting anyone to happen upon the poor woman.

Her mother's grave appeared as it had on the day of the service, fresh and lonely. She set the lavender on the grass where neither her mother nor a stone existed. If her grave was anything like the widow Sanders's, then all that was left was a casket of clothes. The grave robbers would avoid transportation if they were caught with a nude corpse.

Laurel shuddered and hugged her middle. She didn't know why she had come today, but she needed something. A chasm occupied her chest and every drop of memory from her mother hinted at making the gap that much smaller. It would never heal, but at least the pain would dull.

The crunch of leaves alerted her to someone's presence. As she peered back, she expected the Reverend to appear, but instead, a stranger stood no more than ten feet away. She shifted around, forgetting her purpose.

A shock of black hair fell to his shoulders, and his sharp stare left her at a loss for words. He held himself with a power and she concluded he was handsome, but even if he were not, the weight of his presence was magnetic.

He held her gaze, but she couldn't grasp the color of his eyes.

She swallowed. "Can I...help you with something?"

His razor stare seemed to dissect her, study her, and unlock her mind. Bare to him, she stumbled in place. With a swift movement, he caught her arm, and she teetered toward him. Her hand landed on his chest.

Her heart pounded in every corner of her body.

"Careful." His voice was smooth, like velvet, but with a higher tone than what she expected. The sound was sweet but warm, like hot cider.

She righted herself and cleared her throat. "I mean to say, who are you?" He had a familiarity about the eyes, but she couldn't place where she had seen him.

A touch of a grin betrayed his humor, but his visage remained stony.

"I'm me. Who are you?"

This time, he coughed out a laugh. "Conner."

"Just Conner?" A spark of recognition floated between them.

He nodded, his eyes scanning her face as though he were waiting for an argument or a hint of memory.

"That's right. Conner." She paused. "Why are you here?" He still possessed that boyhood charm she had fallen for years ago, and yet, she hadn't known him at first.

She hadn't seen Mr. Conner Woodward since he was a young man, though he was years older than her. They had been distant as children, him being the lord's only son and she the cabinetmaker's daughter. Conner's father would never approve of their relationship, but that hadn't stopped them one summer morning when they met in the forest off the graveyard.

"What does one usually do in graveyards? I came to pay my respects."

She stood aside. "Then by all means." She made a sweeping gesture with her hand.

He stepped forward and stopped. "I seem to be turned around." His gaze swept the area before him. "Can you direct me to the Woodward crypt?"

She was startled, but she was quick to regain her composure. Nobody had visited the Woodward crypt since she could remember.

She forced a smile and faced away before it faltered. "This way."

Laurel stopped around the graves, sensing his gaze

on her back. Her shoulder blades pinched together as she fought the sensation. It wasn't until the towering, unmistakable crypt came into view that he spoke.

"Thank you. I haven't been here in years."

She realized she was staring at the structure. *Laurel, you fool. Get it together.*

His eyes pinned her down again.

She bit her lip. "I've always thought it was impressive." What was she saying?

"Impressive? I suppose it is."

She looked down at the lavender left clenched in her hand. She had meant the rest for Mrs. Boswell. Laurel shoved the flowers toward him.

He blinked down at them. Laurel licked her lips.

"For your loved one."

Again, a smile teased at his lips, and he bowed his head. "I appreciate the gesture, but don't you need them?"

The lavender fell limp in her hand. "Nuh…nuh…no." She avoided that sharp stare.

"Hmm. Then it's only fair you place them. Come with me."

She couldn't find the words to protest. Hadn't she always wanted to enter the crypt? Ever since she was a child, she had imagined something mysterious went on beyond the locked door. The secrets had eluded her, but that didn't mean she couldn't pretend.

He pulled a key the length of her forefinger from his greatcoat and fit it in the lock. To her surprise, the creak and groan of the door came with ease, and he shoved it inward.

She gave him one last look and stepped into the crypt, but it wasn't dipped in shadows and cobwebs the way she had pictured. A light shone through a stained-glass window, throwing a cascade of colors over the stone floor. The walkway was interrupted halfway with a staircase that spun below.

"After you, madam."

A giggle escaped her lips, and she slapped a hand over her mouth. "You must know I don't do this every day." She was rambling again.

"Of course."

She brushed her fingertips over the stone walls as she made for the top of the stairs. "It's beautiful." Her eyes grazed the stone, marble, where the lights of the window reflected from the floor.

"Beautiful as death." He shook his head.

She gave him a pointed look. "I mean the window."

"I know."

Laurel tightened her lips, hoping to shut whatever idiotic thing she might say next. She pushed a mahogany lock behind her ear and took a step downward. Dust scattered with each fall of her boots, and by the time they reached the lower floor, a cloud had formed before them.

She had walked into a void. The light from above refused to penetrate the crypt below. A whoosh of light erupted in the chamber from the lantern Conner had carried from outside, which was set aside for such occasions. Dull gray stone blocks lined the way where graves were set into deep chambers.

The dry air hindered her breathing and she sneezed into the dusty passage.

"Is this what you were expecting?"

She was thankful the light wouldn't reveal her

blush. "No."

"I'm sorry to disappoint you."

"No, that's not it at all. It's more than I could have imagined." She laid a hand on his arm but snatched it away when he noticed it. "It's peaceful."

Conner read her face in the low light. "Right."

He strode forward, not watching to see if she followed. Her heart sank and she tightened her grip on the lavender. Their footsteps were the only evidence of life.

She studied his form as he walked ahead. His backside flexed as he advanced.

He peered back at her and her gaze danced away. "We're almost there." Amusement colored his tone.

"Where is here?"

"Here." He stopped before a space outlined in stone. They were well under the church. It was no wonder there were no other crypts in the graveyard. The Woodward crypt took up the majority of the space.

The space Conner indicated was like any other. Below the stone frame there was a small plaque that read "Margaret Woodward", Conner's mother. Laurel grasped for words but settled on setting the lavender in the space before the coffin.

She tightened her lips over her teeth as she stared at the name.

"I was sorry to hear about your mother," Conner said.

His words beckoned her tears and one slid down her face.

"It isn't easy." He grasped her hand and squeezed.

The tears streamed down her face, and she shook her head. The warmth of his palm lifted from hers and he pressed a hand to her shoulder. "It doesn't get any easier." He dropped his hand and exhaled.

Laurel closed her eyes and took a deep breath. When she opened them, Conner had moved on, leaving an empty space where his warmth had been.

She shifted and found his gaze across the walkway. "What are you doing here?"

"Keeping a promise."

"I don't mean the crypt. What are you doing in Tenwich?"

The lantern's light outlined the creases around his eyes. "Yes, I know." He started for the stairs, and she rushed to keep up with him before the only light disappeared. She had never known Conner to be sentimental, but she supposed most people were when it came to death.

Conner stopped to lock the crypt door and a wind stirred up, whipping his dark strands into his eyes. He pushed the strands away, which did nothing for the sadness in their depths.

She wished it was summer again, back when they had only themselves to worry about. Conner had been home from school and Laurel had spent her days in the sun, collecting freckles her mother scolded her over.

Laurel's mahogany hair floated around her, and Conner reached up to push it into some semblance of order. The action hit her like a cannonball to her stomach. A spark of recognition widened his eyes.

She held her breath, but they weren't children anymore. He wasn't about to take those last few inches and find her lips. This wasn't a game. They were two adults from two completely different families. Nothing could recreate that first kiss, and though her lips tingled, waiting for the action, she stepped back.

Without another word, Conner turned on his heel, leaving her to her memories and the regret that clouded them.

Chapter 3

The sun slid down the sky and hid past the horizon. Laurel set aside the shroud she sewed and found her father hammering the last nails of a fresh coffin. He wiped his brow and eyed her with a slack jaw.

"You're not coming with me."

Laurel made a guttural sound at the back of her throat. "And why not?"

"People already have ideas about you. No use giving them something else to gossip about." He settled the coffin against the wall.

"Let them talk. I want to help."

He shook his head. "There are no fresh graves today. It's doubtful we will catch them."

"You're making excuses. Why don't you want my help?" Laurel's fists knotted in her skirts.

"Laurel, you're a lady."

She sputtered. "Allie helps you with business. Why can't I help with this?"

He rubbed a hand over his face. "Your mother would never forgive me if something happened to you."

"I don't remember Mother wanting me to be a recluse."

His face hardened. "You know your mother loved you and wanted to protect you. The last few years have been hard, I know, but she was still your mother, and she wanted what was best for you."

She sighed. "I know. I'm sorry. I just miss her."

"Then you'll honor her memory and stay here." His gaze held hers until she glanced away.

She slouched in on herself. "Be careful."

Her father met her halfway across the workshop and wrapped his arms around her. "You're a good girl."

She gave him a weak smile. "Are you ready?"

"My dear, I'm always ready." He laughed and released her from his grasp.

Laurel let out a long breath and left him to prepare for his long walk around the perimeter of the graveyard. She found her older sister, Allie, cleaning up after dinner. Instead of helping her with the dishes, Laurel dropped down at the table and propped her head in her hands.

Allie ignored Laurel's dejected state. "I heard you went into the Woodward crypt today."

Laurel dropped her hands onto the table. "How could you possibly know that?" As far as she knew, nobody had seen her and Conner enter the crypt, and she hadn't told anyone. "Did you talk to Conner?"

Allie glanced back at her with a small smile. "No."

Laurel steepled her hands on the table. "Well, you're right."

Her sister's smile widened. "I know I'm right. Why did you want to go in there? Wait, don't tell me, you were curious."

Laurel arched a brow. "If you know all this anyway, why are you asking?"

Allie set the final dish down and faced Laurel. "You know Lord Tenwish wouldn't appreciate you in their family's crypt. It's private, like sneaking into their bedroom."

Laurel waved a hand. "It is not."

"How did you feel when someone took mother?"

"Like I want to kill them." Laurel shook her head. "It's not the same."

"Tell that to the Woodwards."

"But Conner was the one who took me in there."

Allie settled down next to her at the table. 'What do you know about Conner? He's never cared what his father thinks."

"You're right, but Conner is a different person now."

Allie swung her wheat-colored braid over her shoulder. "Not that different."

Her sister was always right. It wasn't a thing of pride. Allie always knew about things. Allie refused to open up about her knowledge and would only share if the time suited her. Her sister's abilities were kept secret in hopes Allie wasn't treated differently than anyone else.

Allie's soft features brightened when she smiled at Laurel.

"Don't look at me like that. It's not going to happen. Even if I wanted it to, he is well above my station."

"Stranger things have happened."

"Not in Tenwich."

"Don't count him out, Laurel. He would make a good friend."

She shot to her feet. "What is he even doing here? Did the Lord fall ill?"

Allie tsked. "His home is here, not in Oxford."

"Yes, but—"

"He's here now, that's what matters." Allie gave

19

her a stern look. "When are you going out?"

Laurel thrust her hands on her hips. "When father can't hear me."

"Take a scarf with you."

Laurel snorted. "You know I will."

Allie sounded more and more like a mother as time passed, but she was still Allie. Still the sister who tolerated her eccentricities. "Also, watch your step."

It was another cryptic Allie warning. Most days she managed to heed Allie's warnings, but tonight she was almost guaranteed to trip with the raised roots and the almost hidden stones of the forest edge. It wasn't so much a warning as it was an assumption.

Allie rose from her place and finished the few remaining chores. Laurel sat silent, waiting on the telling sounds about the house. It wasn't until Allie said good night that Laurel ventured into the yard.

Her boots kicked up dirt as she took the shortcut through their garden. The path wound past their property and continued to a vacant field on the outskirts of the churchyard. She gripped her pistol in one hand and a lantern in the other as she neared the churchyard.

A low light swung in the distance and Laurel elected to search the area they found Mrs. Boswell. She lowered her light, keeping it hidden behind trees and stones. If she could see her father's lantern, he could see hers. If he suspected she had gone against his wishes, the night was over for her.

The forest beyond the graveyard seemed to have its own gravitation. It was the kind of thing that kept Allie from the graveyard but drove Laurel toward it. Vines twisted and grew among the trees, bringing trunks alive with leaves. What was left of the older stones rose and fell on the forest floor.

Her heart fluttered as she stared at each familiar etching. Her ancestors were buried near here, but there was no one to remember their faces. Only their names gave them away. For once, she wished her family had a crypt like the Woodwards. Their history was laid out in neat rows, while hers were scattered, some nameless and forgotten.

As familiar as she was with the graveyard, the area was a different story at night. Distances were warped and she traversed the border with wary steps. Time stretched out with the sunless sky. It must have been an hour before she came around back to the forest. Her father's lantern was out of sight.

Her face was numb from cold, and her boots squeezed her toes. She rubbed her hands together and started home. An owl called overhead, stopping her advance. She held her breath, and when her breath cleared, her hearing opened up.

A creak reverberated through the silence.

The crypt.

Laurel drew her pistol and bolted over the graves. Each step brought a stabbing pain into her feet from her boots. She gritted her teeth and sped up. Her feet wouldn't stop her. Nobody would steal from her graveyard again.

She slowed at the sight of the crypt door swinging back and forth. Creeping forward with her pistol raised, she scanned the area. Finding the way clear, she muttered a curse under her breath. Maybe the wind had knocked the door open. Conner might not have closed the door completely.

She lowered her pistol when the door slammed into

her backside, throwing her into the crypt. Her lantern flew ahead, going out. She climbed to her knees and another gust of wind slammed the door shut.

"Damn it."

A faint trace of the moon through the stained glass was her only light.

She crawled to the lantern, each movement a test of the stone floor. Her now loose hair tumbled in front of her, and she pushed it back each time it fell. She brushed her hands over the ground, hoping to collide with the light.

Her skirts caught under her foot, and she was yanked sideways. The stone crunched beneath her.

"Damn it to hell."

She rolled to her other side and brushed her hands over her gown. She hissed as glass sliced over her palm.

A laugh bubbled in her throat, and it built until her side ached. She pulled her injured hand against her breast. She leaned her head back as though in prayer and closed her eyes.

Hurried steps rained over the stairs and light bounced toward her.

She swept out a hand, hoping to connect with her lost pistol.

A lantern loomed before her, and she raised her injured hand to block out the shine that assaulted her eyes.

"You're bleeding," came the voice beyond the lantern.

Her throat tightened. "Don't come any closer. I'm armed." Never mind she hadn't located her pistol.

"You're armed?" The voice held a hint of humor.

"What do you need with a gun in a crypt? Are you worried about vampires?"'

"Don't be childish."

"I'm not the one who comes armed to a crypt." He lowered the lantern, revealing his face, Conner. Of course, the man had the key.

"What are you doing out here?"

"I could ask you the same."

"I'm trying to prevent robberies."

His eyes widened. "Does your father know you're out here?"

Laurel bit her lip.

"He doesn't." He sighed. "Were you lying about being armed? Tell me you aren't armed."

"I'm not. I dropped it."

He set his lantern down and crouched next to her. "Well, I don't see the gun. Let me look at your hand."

"Can't this wait? We're standing in a crypt."

"So, you are afraid of vampires?" He chuckled.

"I am not. They don't exist."

"That you know of." He peeled her glove away, revealing a red ribbon against her palm.

Despite the pain, his touch tingled over her fingers. She swallowed and clenched her teeth, anticipating his touch.

"It's a shallow cut. You were lucky." He got to his feet.

"Thank you."

"For what? It needs to be bandaged. I can take care of that when I have supplies." He lifted his lantern again and stopped. "You were out there looking for grave robbers?"

"They took my mother."

23

He shook his head. "You're lucky they didn't take you too. Watchers are killed for less. It's one more body they have after they strip you of your clothes to avoid transportation."

"I was armed."

"We've covered that." He met her eyes, and a shiver went up her spine. "Does your father know you have a pistol?"

She folded her arms in front of her. "He gave it to me."

"He what?" Conner blinked at her.

"He taught me to use it too."

"Did he teach you not to go after robbers? They could be armed too."

A flush crept into her cheeks. "What does it matter to you?"

"I'd rather your pretty face wasn't ruined."

Her mouth froze open and then, she snapped it closed.

"Besides, your father needs you."

It wasn't exactly the truth. Her father and Allie would do fine without her. They had their own world, which supported itself. She was outside of it. However much she helped, she couldn't seem to join the rhythm of their home.

"Fine, but why were you out here?"

"Couldn't sleep."

"So, you decided to visit the graveyard and have a look at your loved ones? I'm not sure how that would help you sleep."

The side of his lip turned up. "Seemed as good a time as any."

He was either lying or he was the strangest person

she had ever encountered. She supposed she was right there with him. After all, she was a woman walking at night in the graveyard with a pistol. It didn't get much stranger.

"Never mind." She stretched out her legs and grasped her injured hand in her skirts. "I need to get back."

Her father must have returned by now, and if he noticed she was missing, he would likely take away her pistol and give her horse duty. As much as she loved horses, she didn't love shoveling after them.

He shook his head all the way to the crypt door. "Wasn't this open?"

"The wind shut it."

He yanked on the door, but it resisted. "The lock is on the outside. We're trapped in here."

Chapter 4

"What do you mean we're trapped in here?" Laurel's pulse beat as she pushed and tugged at the door in frantic bursts.

"Relax. We'll just have to wait until someone walks by. With all the noise you're making, I'm sure that won't be long."

"What idiot made the door lock from the outside?"

"One that didn't think corpses would mind being locked in."

She snorted. "Visitors are supposed to leave the door open? Just like that?"

He gave her a hard look. "Just like that."

"What if there was a graverobber in the yard?"

"Then they wouldn't get in."

She rubbed her arms. Had it gotten cold in here? She backed up against the wall, and her gaze darted from side to side. "We could die in here."

He smirked. "Then we would have company."

"Bite your tongue." She groaned.

"I thought you liked graves." He raised a brow.

She sank down to sit on the chilled floor. "Graves, yes. Dark, cramped spaces, no."

Humor sparked in his gray eyes, turning them almost blue in the lantern light. "That's nothing." He waved a hand. "I've heard the crypt is haunted."

She dropped her head against the wall. "Perfect."

"It is said my Great Aunt Merle was nailed into her coffin before her time. When someone complained about the noise, they opened her coffin. There were gouges and blood on the coffin lid and missing fingernails on Merle. Her mouth was open as though she had spent her last breath screaming."

"You aren't helping."

"Some say you can still hear Merle scratching the wood late at night."

"I don't hear anything."

He slid down the wall to sit next to her. "Are you listening?"

It was stupid. Ridiculous, even, but Laurel closed her eyes and listened. The crypt was silent, as silent as, well, the grave. "There's nothing."

"Shhh."

"Really, Conner."

Then, she heard it. The sound was faint, but it was as he said. An insistent scratching, like a cat clawing a tree trunk. Laurel's eyes snapped open.

"You're making that noise."

He raised his palms in front of him and shook his head. "It's Merle."

She slapped his arm. "I don't believe you."

"Believe what you want. You can't say you don't hear it."

She sucked in a breath. "That doesn't mean it's Merle."

He smirked. "Then what is it?"

She twisted her hands together and placed them on her knees to still them. "I don't know. A tree branch?"

"Do you see any trees in here?" He gestured around.

She squinted. "Outside."

"The walls are at least a foot thick. I don't think you can hear anything from outside."

She paled. "Or from inside. Conner, nobody can hear us."

He studied her face. "That's true."

"How will anyone know we're in here? Did you tell anyone where you were going?"

"No. Did you?"

She shook her head. "I never meant to go inside the crypt. I mean, Allie knows I went out to the graveyard but not that I'm here."

Conner grunted. "It's better than nothing."

"How will they know I'm still here? It's a big area to cover. Not to mention the grave robbers."

"What grave robbers?"

"The ones robbing the graves."

He stared at her. "In Tenwich? You weren't kidding?"

"Why would I joke about that?"

"I thought maybe you walked the churchyard at odd hours." He screwed up his lips, drawing her attention to how close he sat. Their shoulders were a bare inch apart.

"I do walk around the graveyard, but not at night."

He scrunched up his nose. "Why?"

"I...I don't know." She had always enjoyed the peace of the graveyard. It reminded her of her maternal grandmother, who she could sit with for hours and say nothing. It was the kind of companionship she craved, and the corpses couldn't talk back. They couldn't reject her, use her, or criticize her. At least they couldn't in her experience.

She shrugged. "I guess it makes me less lonely." She didn't know why she said it but once the words were out, she couldn't take them back. He didn't need to know she was lonely. Of course, if they died in here, it wouldn't matter.

"I'm sorry."

"For what?"

It was his turn to shrug. "That you have to spend time with the dead to feel alive."

Her jaw slackened. He was right. The times she felt like herself, like she mattered, she was in a graveyard. "You must think I'm mad."

A hint of a smile crossed his lips. "Not mad. A bit odd, but we all have our own strange habits."

"If that's the case, what is yours?"

He chuckled. "I lure strange women into crypts."

She frowned. "I'm strange now?"

"That's what bothered you? Not the luring?" He chuckled. The sound woke a smile on her face as it invoked a memory of them joking and laughing in the sun.

She lowered her lashes. "Not so much strange as a stranger."

"You're not a stranger, and you know it."

"Conner, it's been a long time."

His gaze fell to her lips. His thoughts must have echoed hers. The kiss they had shared so long ago. It was her first kiss, her only kiss, but it was a kiss that shook her life up and erased everything she thought she knew about herself.

Their past waved between them like a banner, and she didn't know if she should back away or lean in. It had been too long. Years. Yet, her skin tingled, and her stomach was crammed in knots. All for Conner.

He cleared his throat and laid a hand against the wall as he found his feet. "I think you're right about dying in here."

"That's not reassuring."

"Why don't I hoist you out of that window?" He nodded to the stained glass.

"No. No. No. No. No. We would have to break it. That window must be hundreds of years old."

"It is, but we could die in here. It's just a window, and I can replace it."

She stood. "What would your father say?"

"He wouldn't know. He never comes out here."

"That's convenient," she muttered to herself. "All right, if that's what we have to do."

Laurel yelped as he lifted her onto his shoulders without warning. She weaved as she sat with his head between her legs. Heat pooled low in her belly and her breath caught in her throat. "I would appreciate it if you didn't tell anyone about this." Her words came out on a gasp.

He chuckled and his breath made the inside of her thighs tingle.

She forced her concentration on the window and tried not to think of the colors as the moonlight bounced through them. She sucked in a breath and slammed her fist into the glass. Nothing.

"Harder. It's held up for hundreds of years."

"This would be easier if I could kick."

"Just keep trying."

She studied the glass, her gaze settling on a yellow rose near the top. She struck the pane; it trembled under the blow but refused to break.

"Harder and do it quickly so you don't cut yourself."

She bit her lip to keep from laughing. "You act as though you have experience."

He was quiet for a moment. "Not much."

She shifted on his shoulders and reached closer to the window. "Shield your eyes. This one is going to count."

"Are you ready?"

"I'm always ready."

He didn't get a chance to reply when the force of her fist shattered the glass in a kaleidoscope of color. Conner staggered backward and Laurel weaved. He steadied her with his hands on her thighs.

Laurel placed her hands on his and warmth traveled through their gloves. If someone were to see them, her reputation would be in pieces like the window. Conner inched closer to the window.

"You're going to have to lift me higher," she said.

"Hold on." He lowered her to the ground and shrugged out of his coat. "Here."

"What do I need this for?"

He gave her a blank stare. "So you don't cut yourself getting out. And here." He handed her the key. "Unlock the door for me."

He created a cradle with his hands, and she stepped into it. With a swift flex of his arms, the broken window appeared before her. She punched out the remaining glass with the coat wrapped around her fist and set the coat over the base of the window, which she hoped would protect her from any stray shards.

She grasped the edge of the window, coat and all, and pulled herself up with help from Conner, who had a view beneath her skirts. Laurel scrambled on her stomach.

"You might want to hurry unless you want me to see more than your birthmark."

She squeaked and flung herself through the window. She landed on her hands, sending a sharp pain through her injured hand. Laurel glared down at him. "You had no right."

He leaned against the wall. "I didn't have much choice."

Heat flooded her cheeks. "You could have closed your eyes."

"And let you fall? I wasn't going to do that. Don't be embarrassed. It looks like a flower."

A flower that was painted on her upper thigh. She choked on her words.

"I have a mind to leave you down there."

"But you won't."

She shot him a sharp look. "How can you be so sure?"

"It isn't like you to hold grudges."

She tapped a finger on her lip. "Well, I might just start."

"Funny. Now, come open the door."

"I'll think about it." She walked out of view of the window and stopped. What if she did leave him down there? He would be found eventually but that could take weeks or even months. As embarrassed as she was, she couldn't let him suffer for something he couldn't help.

She pondered his release as she made her way to the door, taking her time as she fiddled with the key. She wouldn't leave him, of course, but letting him doubt his freedom felt like revenge enough.

She popped the key into the lock and turned. The door swung open, revealing a smiling Conner.

"I knew you wouldn't leave me."

His words rammed into her chest. Wasn't that what he said all those years ago? He wouldn't leave her? She remembered all those school holidays when he hadn't returned. This was the first time they met after their summer together—it was like he didn't recognize her. They had become two different people, older and less foolish.

His face fell when he saw her worn expression. "Listen, about your mother."

She stared numbly ahead.

"I'll help you find the grave robbers."

"You don't have to." She handed him off the key.

"I know, but I want to." His lips tilted up in an attempt at a smile. "Besides, I have a lot of free time these days."

"But at night?"

"I haven't slept well in years."

"I'm sorry, but I'm not sure I can search. My father doesn't know I'm out here. I was trying to help him."

He nodded. "I see, but what I don't understand is why is it stopping you? It didn't tonight, and it hasn't in the past. You never cared what people thought of you."

"If we do this, there will be rumors."

"There always are."

"Why do you want to help me?"

He shrugged. "It's the least I can do since you lost your mother." And she assumed he knew what it was like to lose that part of you. Though he didn't say it, the words were there gathered in front of them.

I've missed you, she wanted to say. Though their

33

friendship had been brief, it was close. Their lives had intertwined for that one perfect moment. As much as she missed him, she knew they couldn't go back. Too many things stood between them.

She started to refuse him, but instead, her lips betrayed her. "When do we start?"

Chapter 5

In her haste to return to her room, Laurel neglected to take care with the back door, and it slammed behind her. She flinched, but her efforts wouldn't have mattered as Allie burst into the kitchen.

"Where were you?"

"The graveyard like I said."

"We've been worried. We could have used your help."

Laurel's brows raised. "Help with what?"

Allie glared at her. "Someone chased father down in the cemetery. He took a fall trying to escape the madman. You're lucky you didn't encounter anyone. The doctor is on the way."

Laurel gasped and pushed past Allie, moving to the front parlor. Her father sat on the worn blue sofa. His foot was propped on cushions on the wooden stool. His years seemed to weigh on him as he gazed at her with creased eyes.

She picked out a blade of grass from his mussed, gray hair. "I'm sorry, father. I should have been there."

He frowned back at her. "I told you to stay behind. If they had caught you—"

"I know, and I would have, but there is so much ground to cover."

He narrowed his eyes. "The only thing that scared my attacker away was my pistol. I was lucky to get a hold of it in time. You might not have been so lucky. I don't want you in the cemetery."

"You don't know the graveyard like I do." She worried her lip between her teeth. Her father had been in real danger, and she hadn't been there to help.

Her father sighed. "Your mother was right. I shouldn't have allowed you to spend so much time there. It's one thing for a woman to sew shrouds for extra pay but quite another to allow her to spend time with the dead. I'm only glad the Reverend noticed your mother's slipper before you did. That would have brought a world of headache."

She wanted to ask why it would make a difference, but the hard look in his green gaze told her enough. Her determination would never have let her stop searching once she had found the shoe, and she would probably be halfway to London by now on one of her hunches.

Laurel settled her gaze on her father's leg. "Does it hurt? Is there anything I can do?"

"Not as it did before your sister treated me. Don't trouble yourself."

"But, father, don't you see that you need me more than ever? Allie can help during the day, and I can watch the graveyard at night. I'll be safe with my pistol. I don't want anyone else to get hurt."

"Laurel," —he grasped her hand— "don't you dare."

"It's no trouble."

"I would rather a corpse was stolen than you getting hurt. What kind of parent would I be if I didn't protect you? Stay home and help your sister." He dropped her hand.

Her hand swung at her side. "I don't have to do it alone. I have help."

"The young ladies of your acquaintance shouldn't

be out late either." He shook his head. "I've had enough of this. Go to bed. I won't have you endangering yourself for a corpse."

"Not a lady, father. Conner Woodward offered to help me."

His eyes grew round. "You can't be serious. You are going to stay here. No more roaming the graveyard. The only places I want to hear of you going are the market and church."

Her mouth dropped open. "What's wrong with Conner?"

"Hunting the graveyard at night with that fiend is the worst sort of gossip, and I don't want to lose you too."

He shifted his leg and grunted. "Besides, I want you married by this time next year. And being found out at night with Connor could hinder a betrothal. I'm serious, Laurel. The family needs you to marry. We don't have the luxury of waiting any longer. Our finances are scarce as it is. Tonight, I came close to being beaten to death. I won't be around forever, and I'd like to see you settled."

"That's not fair. Allie isn't married."

"Allie is an asset to the business. What do you do? Waste your time inside your head making up fairy tales. You need a household of your own. A purpose. I'm tired of your excuses. You will marry and that's final."

Laurel's stomach knotted. "If it pleases you."

"It would please me if you got out of my sight. I don't want to hear another word."

She turned on her heel, nearly colliding with Allie, who stood in the doorway to the hall. Laurel bunched up her skirts as she rushed up the stairs. Her father had only hinted at her marrying before. It had been her mother who had tried to wed her off. This was the first time he had ordered her to do anything. Why now of all times, and what did Conner have to do with it?

Laurel threw herself on her old bed, not bothering to undress. Why did things have to change? She wanted her old world back. Her old room, her routine, and her mother. Tears spilled from her eyes. She wanted her mother.

She huffed out a breath and wiped at her face. Her mother wouldn't want to see her cry. No, she would rub Laurel's shoulders and tell her to get on with the day because the day wouldn't stop to wait for her. Her parents would want her married, and she would have to do her best.

Her father was right, he had risked death tonight. Who could have wanted to hurt her father? H was an upstanding citizen of Tenwich. People liked him. At least, most people liked him. He must have interrupted the graverobber who had chased her father down with a shovel. He had been close. She didn't want to throw away their chances, but now, she had to locate a husband.

How hard could it be to find a husband?

A laugh bubbled up in her throat and she couldn't stop it from shaking her body. Laurel find a husband? The drab graveyard girl who lived in her head. Funny that she didn't have any suitors.

The more she thought about it, the more ridiculous it sounded. Her? Married? And with children? That would be one benefit to starting a family. She found that children loved her stories as much as she did. If she was going to do this, she would do it right.

First, she needed to learn to cook. She rubbed away the rest of her tears and straightened her skirts. Her nightgown was in her parent's room from the night before, but since her father's fall, she wasn't sure he would want to drag himself up the stairs regardless of his feelings about his old room.

Laurel took each step with care, not wanting to be lectured again. Her silence revealed voices speaking low in the parlor.

"You can't just give up on her," Allie said.

"I'm not giving up. She needs to grow up or she'll be on the streets after I pass."

A stone lodged in her throat. She had no idea her father thought of her that way.

"You know I'll always look after her."

Laurel had to hold herself back from running to hug her sister. At least she could count on her in case she failed to secure a husband, which was more than likely the case. Her only suitor had been the butcher's son, who had a weak chin and a habit of picking his nose, but even he was able to secure a spouse.

Her father must have made some gesture in reply while it was quiet.

"You shouldn't need to."

"Did you tell her about Mr. Cross?"

"Huh." He paused. "Mr. Cross doesn't need her burdening him either. You will start your own family, but you know I won't force you to marry."

Mr. Cross was her father's apprentice, who had fallen for Allie the first day he set his gangly body in their workshop. He must have finally proposed. What she didn't expect was Allie's acceptance. Of course, her sister had known all along, but she hadn't given so much as a hint of her knowledge.

Mr. Cross was a kind man, and she had no doubt he would take her in, but he tended to be strict. Any freedom she exercised now would disappear if he was the head of the household. Already her father would erase some of her joy. What more did the world want from her?

Laurel crept past the parlor door and fetched her nightgown from the master bedroom. She was halfway to the stairs when her father's voice spoke up again.

"Don't baby her. If she isn't married by Christmas, we'll have to find her a situation somewhere."

Her sister scoffed. "Doing what?"

"I don't know. She would make an acceptable maid."

"The Woodwards might need help."

The silence that fell was absolute, but she thought she could hear the roar that preceded her father's words.

"No daughter of mine will set foot at the Woodward's estate. If I'm dead and buried and you go against my wishes, I will come back and haunt you until the day you die. Then, I will disturb your eternal rest for the rest of eternity. Do you hear me?"

"Yes, but why?"

"Never you mind." He paused. "Help me into my bed. We'll discuss this more tomorrow."

Allie must have hesitated when he spoke again. "I'll be fine. If your mother haunts anyone, it will be the ones who took her body. My hard memories can stay with me until I heal. The stairs are too much for me now." Laurel flinched. He would stay in his old room he had shared with mother.

The stool scraped against the floor, and Laurel

bolted up the stairs two at a time. The thud with each step seemed to echo off the walls. She winced with every creak and groan of the wood.

She balled up her nightgown and threw it in the corner. How was she supposed to find a husband between the market and church? She would cross all the same men. The same married men and the ineligible bachelors that even Allie wouldn't find acceptable.

Laurel had no qualms about being a maid. Although cleaning was one of the few things she was good at, she hated feeling compelled to choose a profession. True, she had been given plenty of time to find her own way. Yet, between caring for her mother while her father and sister worked at the cabinet business and getting lost in her stories and shrouds, she hadn't had a chance.

If years of caring for her mother had taught her one thing, the medical profession wasn't for her. That left her with a maid or governess. She did enjoy children, but her lack of experience would scare away her prospects. At least maids could make mistakes without endangering children. Usually.

Then there was the lack of opportunity in the parish. Aside from the Woodward estate, there weren't many families that could afford a maid. What did her father have against the Woodwards? This was the first she had heard of it.

Granger Woodward, Lord Tenwich was a prosperous landowner, and though he was disagreeable to her the one time they met, the people of Tenwich considered it an honor to serve Lord Tenwich and his son. That is, except for her father.

As far as she knew, her father and Conner's had

never crossed paths unless it was in church, which was unlikely since Tenwich was too reclusive to bother with conversation. To her knowledge, Lord Tenwich had never used their services. The Woodwards ordered most of their goods from foreign countries.

She extinguished her lantern and bundled herself in bed. The nights had grown colder and longer, and though it gave the robbers some advantage, they were left with the frozen ground over the coming months. Now would be the time to be on guard.

They had a brief window to collect corpses, and she sensed that whatever they used the corpses for would need a regular supply of bodies. What then would happen? A chill passed over her lower spine, but she ignored it.

You're going to get yourself killed, Laurel.

Still, she knew what she had to do. She would leave the robbers to whoever wanted them and find herself a husband before she spent the rest of her life emptying chamber pots and scrubbing pans.

As soon as she woke, she would make her way to church and speak to every stranger who even resembled a bachelor. When she was done, she would converse with the elderly mothers, grandmothers, and aunts. Someone had to know about potential suitors for her.

Her decision was made, and a smile creased her cheeks. She dozed off thinking of babies and peaceful evenings but this soon turned into a nightmare as she dreamed Conner's Aunt Merle chased her through the graveyard, screaming that Laurel had stolen her hands.

Laurel came awake the next morning, red handprints on her throat from where the corpse had grabbed her.

Chapter 6

"He did what?" Laurel's best friend, Maya Meadows, sat across from her in the parlor as they sewed their respective work.

"He described my birthmark." Laurel shivered at the memory.

"How did you allow such a thing?" Maya curled up her lip.

Laurel swiped at Maya with the shroud she was working on. "I didn't allow anything. I didn't have much of a choice."

Maya shook her head. "I wish I had seen your face. Conner Woodward looking up your skirts. There are worse things."

The two tall windows lit the parlor, allowing the midday sun to shed its brightness. They sat in green padded chairs that flanked one of the windows. A finch sat singing on a tree beyond the windowpane as though it would join them in their work.

"You have all the fun." Maya grinned. "Grave robbers and Conner?"

"Maya, there was nothing fun about it. My mother is missing, and someone tried to murder my father."

"And you'll find her. Luckily, your father got away with a sprain."

"I'm glad someone has faith in me."

Maya pointed her needle at Laurel. "How can your

father possibly think you will find a match by Christmas? It takes forever to find a decent match in Tenwich. At least for us, anyway."

Laurel threw up her hands, nearly dropping the fabric. "I don't know. He's being unreasonable. I wish mother was here. She had more sense than that."

Maya frowned. "I'm sorry, dear."

Laurel sighed. "He should at least let me finish mourning. As much as I'm tired of black, I owe mother that much."

Maya patted her hand. "Agreed."

Silence passed between them as they thought over Laurel's predicament. Maya caught her gaze. "So, when are you sneaking out?"

Laurel's eyes scanned the room in case someone had materialized. "Tonight. I can't waste any time. Everyone in Tenwich knows my father was out watching when he was attacked. Besides, Tag Everett took a spill from his stallion." She waved the shroud.

"Poor Tag." Maya frowned. "He shouldn't have been drinking."

"When was he ever not?"

They shook their heads in unison.

"So does this mean you get to go to the Harvest festival?"

Laurel perked up. "Maybe so. I'll have to ask."

"Good. I didn't want to go alone this year." A lock of tightly coiled red hair bounced in Maya's excitement.

"I love my mother, but she would want me to go. I'm sure of it. She always said crying was a waste of time."

"She was right, of course. She and Allie." Maya

didn't finish what she was going to say. She didn't have to. Laurel's mother and sister seemed to know things others could only guess at. They both had refused to talk about it. It was another way Laurel was excluded from the family.

"Listen, don't tell anyone about Conner."

Maya scoffed. "Why would I do such a thing?"

"Please, Maya."

Maya raised a brow. "You said nothing happened."

"It didn't, but you know how it is. With all the details, anyone could come to their own conclusions about it. It's bad enough my father knew I snuck out."

"Are you going to take his offer to help?"

Laurel's green gaze widened. "Why would I do that?"

Maya sported a smug smile. "He was all you could think about the last few summers. Now's your chance."

"Don't be ridiculous. I'm not losing my head to Conner Woodward."

"There are worse ways to lose your virginity."

"You're horrible. What would happen if I got pregnant? I don't even want to think about it. You shouldn't either." Laurel held up a finger when Maya meant to speak. "I don't care that everything worked out for you. Not everyone is as lucky. I don't want to end up like those mistresses strapped down with babies they can't take care of."

Maya rolled her eyes.

"You know it would happen. The Woodwards would never tolerate a bastard."

"I see you've given this some thought."

Laurel's face blazed. "In passing."

"You're interested." Maya clapped her hands

together, dropping her needlework. "It's too perfect."

"Stop it. Nothing good could come out of a relationship with Conner. He's too good for me."

Maya bunched up her freckled nose. "You're worth a hundred Conners and you know it."

Laurel's grin crowded her features. "You know what I mean."

"I still think you should consider him as a bedmate. How could anyone resist that stunning profile?"

Laurel made a face, sticking out her tongue. "You have the oddest notions." Regardless of what she said, Laurel agreed with her friend. "I'm doing well without him."

"If you say so."

Yet, he hadn't bothered to see her until he had no choice. She was left like a shroud dangling on the laundry line, floating away when forgotten. "It doesn't matter," she lied.

Maya cleared her throat. "In any case, I'm sure we'll see him at the festival."

"Assuming I can go."

"If your father doesn't approve, leave it to me. I'll say 'Mr. Atwell, your daughter is in desperate need of fun and, ahem, sexual satisfaction. Can't you see you're sheltering her?'"

Laurel slapped a hand over her mouth. "You wouldn't dare."

Maya slumped her shoulders. "No, I wouldn't. Think about it though. If he wants you married off so badly, he will give you the opportunity. You can't meet anyone sitting around sewing shrouds." Her lips twisted up at Laurel's latest project.

"In any case, I need to pay a few calls." Maya rose

from her seat. "Remember to get out there. No more daytime graveyard strolls unless you want to marry a corpse."

Laurel rose with her. "You're right."

Maya kissed her cheek and patted her arm. "See you at the festival."

Laurel sighed. She had her doubts about what her father would say. Festival or no festival, she had to get to work. As Maya made her exit, Laurel set down her completed shroud. She straightened her appearance and plastered on her most chastened face. It was time to talk to her father.

To her surprise, her father was receptive to her reasons to attend the Harvest Festival. She suspected he wanted her to stay occupied instead of roaming the graveyard for grave robbers. What he didn't seem to understand was that she had already prepared to search the grounds that night.

When the last of daylight hid behind the hills, she crept down the stairs and snuck through the hallway and out the kitchen door. Her all-black wardrobe worked in her favor, but her lantern would allow others to notice her from far away. She attempted to remedy this by creating a shade out of an unfinished shroud.

She searched for her pistol but came up with nothing and settled on a hunting knife of her father's. It would have to be enough. Her town needed her to safeguard their loved ones. With her father injured, she was one of the few willing and capable of searching the graveyard at night.

She stepped with care over the leaves as they crunched under her boots. At least she would hear the grave robbers before she saw them, but they would also hear her. She sighed and hoisted the lantern higher.

The moon stayed hidden behind clouds, refusing to assist in her plans. A chill crawled over her skin, summoning gooseflesh on her arms. An owl hooted off to her left and her gaze shot in that direction.

A crunch-like thunder sounded behind her, and she flipped around, lantern raised to use as a weapon.

Her arms stopped just in time not to bash Conner Woodward on his pretty head.

She raised a hand to her breast. "Don't do that."

"I thought you were comfortable in the graveyard." Mirth danced in his gaze.

Laurel frowned. "Not when there are grave robbers around."

His eyes, like silver discs in the lantern light, searched her face. "You've seen them?"

She shrugged. "My father saw enough of them, and I'm trying to be careful. They seem to go after fresh bodies usually." She knew her reasoning was weak. As far as she knew, only two of the corpses had been new. How many more were missing she didn't know.

"Here." He held up a pistol, and she flinched.

It took her too long to realize the gun was hers. "Where did you find it?" It was the only thing she could think of to say. Of course, he had found it in the crypt where she had left it. Conner brought the stupid out of her.

Instead of answering, he motioned for her to take it. "I thought I would find you prowling around here."

"You aren't going to tell my father, are you?"

"Why would I do that? We're both adults."

Her green gaze brightened. Nobody had ever mentioned her as an adult. Being an unmarried woman had never given her that title.

He smiled, and warmth pooled from the tip of her nose to her toes. She wanted to kick herself. This was Conner. The man her father wanted her to avoid. The man she wanted nothing more than to sink into.

She shook her head. "You could have come during the day."

"And risk your father knowing I had the pistol?"

So, he did know what her father thought of him, and yet, Conner seemed to wear the dislike like a badge of honor. His eyes shone and crinkled in amusement.

"I don't want to inconvenience you."

"It's no trouble, unfortunately."

She barked out a laugh. "You prefer to be troubled."

"Laurel, you're the best kind of trouble."

Her face heated and she looked away. What was she doing? This could only end badly. She couldn't see herself like Maya, willing to risk it all for a quick tupping. Lauren couldn't deny the shared attraction. It hummed between them like a blazing hearth.

She cleared her throat. "Have you seen anyone?"

"No, and you shouldn't either."

"You know I can't stay at home. This is important."

He sighed. "Which is why you're going to let me help you. It would be irresponsible for me to let you do this alone."

She squared her shoulders. "You aren't *letting* me do anything. I'm an adult, remember?"

"There is a thin line between being an adult and being a fool. What you're planning is a bad idea. Nobody should confront grave robbers alone."

She glared at him. "Fine." She didn't need help, especially not his. She had gone without him for years without trouble. He would be a nuisance, but she could pretend he wasn't there. "On one condition."

"Yes?"

"Nobody hears about this."

"I would say the same to you."

"Conner, I mean it. I don't even want your valet to know. People talk in Tenwich and something like this will ruin me."

"Ruin you? No." He chuckled.

Laurel pointed a finger at his chest. "You don't need to worry about it, but I do. I can't be a spinster. I don't make myself useful as it is."

He waved her concerns away. "You're doing fine."

She snorted. "I'll believe it when I see it." Without waiting for him to respond, she raised her lantern and took off to the right, where the newer graves were nestled along a hill. Their steps rustled the leaves, but they remained otherwise quiet.

However, her mind refused to be silent.

If there were grave robbers that night, they had been scared away by the noise she and Conner had made. Her boot falls had turned to stops as she thought of all the ways Conner could ruin her reputation. It was for the best though, or so she told herself. Conner would be another set of eyes and another pair of ears.

She refused to let him unsettle her. Memories or not, their attraction would be left in the past. A relationship between them couldn't happen, and even a friendship would be unthinkable. Her father would never approve of them even speaking. Not to mention he was the son and heir to Lord Tenwich, and she was a shroud maker with only pennies to her name.

Chapter 7

The rest of their watch passed without event. Laurel kept her distance from Conner, and the graves remained undisturbed.

Although she returned well before dawn, Laurel had little sleep. By the time the Harvest Festival rolled into the day, she could barely keep her eyes open, and every sudden noise made her jerk upright.

The annual Tenwich Harvest Festival was held in October. The church was decorated with fruits and every citizen was invited to the feast. The midday feast was followed by games and dancing. A bonfire towering over Laurel blazed brightly, its flames visible for miles around.

Laurel sat at a long table with her head in her hand. A plate of fresh bread and jam sat before her. Maya picked at the baked apple in front of her.

"Remind me why I came." Laurel met Maya's gaze.

"If you'll wake up, you'll realize you need to find a husband, but really you're here to see Conner."

Laurel's face reddened. "Just the husband part."

Maya swatted at a fly. "I've known you your whole life and finding a husband has always been a low priority."

"Well, it isn't now."

"I told you. You should have slept with him last

night then you wouldn't be so snappish."

"No, but I'd be expecting and hopeless."

"Nonsense. There are ways around it."

Laurel covered her ears and closed her eyes. "Stop talking. I'm not bedding Conner."

Laughter filtered through her hands, and Laurel's eyes snapped open. Her face changed to a vibrant shade of red poppy. Conner stood beside them, carrying a handful of lavender. She didn't dare meet his eyes.

He cleared his throat. "I thought I would repay the favor."

She accepted the bunch and forced herself to smile at him. His lips formed a half-smile. Her heart stuttered and she looked away.

"Thank you," her voice came out in a dry whisper.

"What?" He leaned forward.

She licked her lips and found his gaze again. "Thank you. My mother would have loved them. Don't you think, Maya?" Why did he make her ramble?

Maya giggled and nodded her head. "Beautiful."

"And such a lovely shade of blue. I always wondered why we call it lavender when it's actually blue." *Shut up, Laurel.*

His smile widened. Was he laughing at her? She gave him an even wider smile.

"Laurel was just telling me about last night." Maya tugged on her ear. It was a sure sign she was up to something.

Conner's gaze shifted between them. "Nothing happened."

"I care to differ." Maya tugged on her ear again. "A handsome man like you and our beautiful Laurel out alone in the dark." She paused. "You must have been terrified."

Laurel let out a breath. Maybe her friend wouldn't embarrass her after all.

"It was nothing."

"Nothing? Poor Laurel lost sleep over it. Look at her tired eyes and tell me it was nothing, but still, she's beautiful."

When she got Maya alone, she was going to strangle her.

"She is."

What? He agreed. She had never been called beautiful except by her mother and Maya. In Tenwich, she wasn't known as one of the town's beauties. She was odd Laurel or mad Laurel. He was being polite, that was all.

"You see, Laurel. He agrees with me." Her friend pointed at Conner.

Laurel wanted to melt under the table, but instead, she took a bite of bread to avoid replying. She sensed Conner staring at her, and she looked up from her plate, her face full of food.

He chuckled.

"So, when will the two of you dance?" Maya bit her lip. If it hadn't been the Harvest Festival, her friend wouldn't have asked, but in this particular celebration, class and rank had no meaning. Everyone was equal and even the Woodwards were expected to join in like the rest of Tenwich.

"We don't have to," she blurted out.

"Whenever you're ready," Conner spoke at the same time.

Maya clapped her hands together. "Perfect."

Conner took her hand with a familiarity she hadn't

expected, but it didn't stop her palm from sweating in her glove. When Conner turned toward the other dancers, Laurel scowled at Maya.

I hate you, Laurel mouthed the words.

No, you don't. Maya's face brightened.

Laurel groaned and turned her attention to Conner. She shouldn't be wasting her time dancing with him, but come to think of it, maybe he would encourage other men to approach her. He was the best catch in Tenwich. He just wasn't *her* catch. It was one thing to share a kiss when you were young.

They lined up for the next dance and her pulse thrummed through her veins. She wasn't a good dancer by any stretch of the imagination, but she loved it all the same. When Conner bowed and smiled, her breath caught until the music started.

Laurel stepped and twirled with the rest of her neighbors, but she forgot anyone was there except the smiling face of the man she couldn't have. Her father would scold her later, but for now, her thoughts were on the dance.

She let the music wash over her, filling her up. Every step started and stopped with the realization that Conner danced with her. He could dance with anyone in Tenwich, but he had chosen her. True, it was Maya's doing but he didn't have to agree.

When the dance concluded, Conner's eyes locked with hers. The other dancers moved to switch partners, but Laurel seemed to drift in place. He found her hands and they moved to close the gap between them.

A shout rang up as the bonfire whooshed.

Laurel started and her father frowned at her from across the field. She shook her head at him, knowing she would regret it later.

"Care for another?" Conner's voice was sweet and low. How could she refuse him?

"Yes." She swallowed back the doubt her father had raised. Tonight was for celebration. Tomorrow she would keep her distance.

Laurel laughed as she spun around, the light buzz from a small beer lifting her spirits, while Conner seemed to revert back to the boy she once knew. They were two teenagers enjoying the last of the season and soaking up what was left of the summer.

The moon made a brief appearance, refusing to reveal whether it was full or slivered. The fire cracked and sputtered beside them as their shadows came to dance beside them. The flames lowered and couples left for home. Still, they danced.

It wasn't until the horizon glowed that they stopped. The air had chilled with the absence of the large bonfire. They were one of the three couples who had stayed the night celebrating the harvest.

Laurel's feet and legs throbbed, but her heart was full of laughter. Conner kept his gaze on her as they moved off from the celebration. Wordlessly, they walked to her house. Their smiles mirrored each other, lighting up both of their faces.

"I had a wonderful time," she said as they reached the cottage's front door.

"As did I."

She opened her mouth to speak but he raised a hand.

"Laurel, I think we need to stop watching for the grave robbers."

Her heart pinched. "But why? Someone has to do

it."

"Those people are dead. You're alive. I don't want to see anything happen to you."

Her face heated. "You're in just as much danger as I am."

"That may be, but nobody would miss me."

She shook her head. "I'm sure your father would."

"Aside from being his heir, I doubt he would notice."

"I'm sure that's not true. Everyone speaks highly of you."

His brow arched. "Now that's a lie."

"You're right, my father doesn't like you."

He chuckled. "You risked a lot dancing with me."

She gripped his arm and squeezed. "It won't be all bad, and we'll catch the robbers."

"Laurel," his gaze sharpened, "I was serious before."

"I am too. I want my mother back." She bit down on her lips to keep them from wobbling.

He studied her features and guided her to his shoulder. "She's not coming back."

Tears dampened his shirt, but he didn't pull away. The chasm that was once her heart widened and she sobbed. Every moment she had spent with her mother up to her last days flashed through her mind. Her capable mother was reduced to a helpless shell of herself. Nobody deserved what her mother had gone through.

Her sobs tapered off, and she breathed in the familiar scent of him from so long ago. Spiced cake and cedar. Her heart raced as she realized what they were doing, but she didn't dare move. She tilted her chin up, and his heated stare bored down on her.

"Conner... "

He pressed a finger to her lips and bent the last few inches.

"Laurel, come inside." Her father's voice boomed from the doorway.

She jumped back from Conner, and her face paled.

Later, Conner mouthed.

She gave him a small smile and pivoted on her heel. "I'm coming." She marched into the cottage as Conner took his leave. Laurel found her father off the entryway in the parlor. He sat forward with his elbows resting on his knees.

"Do I need to ask you to explain yourself?"

She gave him a sweet smile. "Well, you don't have to."

He shook his head. "Laurel, I told you to stay away from him."

Her smile fell into a thin line. "Yes, but you didn't say why."

"It doesn't matter why. It only matters that you do as I say." He threw up his hands. "The whole town will be talking about you and him."

"They already do."

His jaw hardened. "Not like this. You can't afford to dally with him."

"We weren't dallying. It was only dancing."

"That's not what it looked like from the window."

Her fists bunched at her sides. "You were spying on me."

He straightened from his chair, which must have cost him when he limped toward her. "You're my daughter. It isn't spying."

She folded her arms. "Then what is it?"

"Enough of this." He grunted. "You will do as I say, or you can find yourself another home."

Her mouth dropped open. "You don't mean that. Mother would never allow it."

"Your mother isn't here. I am."

"I can't believe this." Her mind raced over her options and whirled back to Conner. Was his friendship worth losing her home? They barely knew each other. "Fine. I'll stay away from Conner."

"And the rest of the Woodwards."

She nodded. "All of them."

He backed up to the chair and sat down. "Go to sleep. I expect you'll have quite a headache when you wake up."

Her grin returned and she kissed his forehead.

A knot had formed in her throat, and she attempted to swallow it down. She had barely seen Conner since they were young. What little time they had spent together wasn't enough to fight for. They hadn't talked much, and she was thankful she never got to know the older Conner.

She made her way slowly up the stairs, allowing the wood to creak and groan under her weight. Allie would be up soon to feed the chickens, and Laurel didn't have the energy to be careful. Her lack of sleep the night before and her staying up well past dawn had worn whatever was left of her resistance to sleep.

Tonight, she danced with the most eligible man in Tenwich. They had never switched partners and not from lack of offers. She didn't care what her neighbors thought of her, or at least, that is what she told herself. The Harvest Festival was a break from routine and propriety. When she woke, she would need to throw out her childhood, including Conner Woodward.

The loss of his friendship did have one advantage—she could watch the graveyard without his arguments. She would find out who was stealing bodies and why. Her father wouldn't be pleased with her, but with any luck, he wouldn't find out until she succeeded. She was armed and ready.

Chapter 8

Laurel slept without dreams, only to wake to nightmares. Sunlight burned her eyes, coating her eyelids in red, and she groaned away what was left of her sleep. It was well past midday, and she would have just enough time to complete her chores before dinner.

She rose and donned a wool gown that would serve her well tonight. Last night, she hadn't stopped dancing long enough to feel the increasing chill. She made it to the stairs when voices greeted her.

"We don't know that," the Reverend said.

Laurel bounced down the stairs. "Know what?"

Her father eyed her. "The Reverend thinks we have a body. He wants me to make another community coffin."

Her mouth dried. "But there isn't one?"

Her father shook his head. "Only blood and nobody to claim it. In any case, I suspect someone had too many drinks last night and took a shortcut through the cemetery. Probably cut himself on those brambles on the east side."

"Where was the blood?"

"This is no conversation for a lady," the Reverend interrupted.

She sighed. If the Reverend only knew the conversations she had been included in with her father and sister. Death was present in their lives the way it

61

wasn't in most people's homes. Being a cabinet maker and shroud sewer made death an everyday conversation piece. A little blood meant nothing to her.

Micah Atwell didn't bother to defend her.

"In any case, we need a new coffin. Our old one is barely holding it together. This time, use elm."

"We should have used elm before." Her father shrugged.

The Reverend frowned but didn't admit he had been wrong to cut corners. "I want you to make it, not that slip of a girl you have."

He was referring to Allie. Her sister was proficient at making coffins, but she excelled at cabinet making, much to everyone's disapproval. What the Reverend was proposing wasn't a difficult task, and she suspected he insisted only to get the upper hand.

Her father bowed his head. "Yes, sir."

"And try to keep this one under control." He nodded toward Laurel. The Reverend let himself out.

Mr. Atwell studied her. "If I didn't know you were at the festival all night, I would ask you if you were in the cemetery."

"I know nothing about the blood. It certainly isn't mine."

"You would tell me if you knew." It wasn't a question but came out as a threat. Would she tell him? Probably, but she needed to know where the blood came from first. "Before you ask, he didn't tell me where the blood was, but I suspect it was near the forest. My attacker came from that direction."

Except the blood wasn't necessarily connected to the bodies.

"I don't want to hear of you investigating."

She was already in enough trouble with her father, but that didn't mean she planned to stay home. Her father couldn't search, and she couldn't let them get away with taking her mother's body.

He shuffled back to take his place on a chair. She had seen him in the parlor more times within the past couple of days than she had in years. Allie must be doing the work for now. Guilt squeezed her chest.

"Father, do you need anything?"

He gave her a small smile. "I need you to stay home. I know it isn't in your nature. Go to the market if you must but stay away from the graveyard."

He continued when she hesitated. "Remember to stay away from the Woodwards, Conner especially."

It did seem as though she had gained a selective memory, but instead, she only chose to follow the rules that suited her, and to hell with the consequences. She left her father to his thoughts and went through the motions of her chores. She swept and dusted and checked on the laying hens. She came away with three eggs and a headache from hitting her head on the coop.

She rubbed her head as night descended on them. Allie hadn't returned from the shop, so Laurel stirred the soup and sliced the bread that her sister had set out that morning. They ate, and still no Allie.

It wasn't until she asked that her father explained. "She had plans with Mr. Cross."

"At this hour?"

He raised his brows. "This coming from you?"

"You're right. If she comes back tonight, let her know I'll see her in the morning." She hadn't seen her sister all day and regardless of what her father said, she had started to worry.

"About that," her father paused, "I need to get out of that bed, but for now, you'll have to keep your old room." Of course, memories of her mother troubled him.

"All right." She didn't dare comment on her father's request. She had sensed her mother's presence herself. It must have been exhausting for him. His absence from the search only pushed her further. She needed answers.

As soon as her father settled into bed, she made her calm way through the back door. Lantern held high, she avoided the windows and found the pathway to the graveyard. Her boots had worn it down and tonight was no different. Yet, the air seemed to speak to her as she huddled into herself against the chill.

Something was happening. She could sense the difference in the air. A thin pillar of smoke rose from the forest. Someone had started a fire, but why? There were few forests left in the area and Tenwich was proud of the little group of trees. It was small enough to walk around within a day but large enough to hide something.

She paused to stare ahead, allowing her heart to slow. Laurel was moving too fast, making too much noise under her boot heel. She took a slow step from toe to heel and then another. She considered turning around, getting help, but the fire was small as though it was contained. A campfire maybe, but who would camp in the forest?

Grave robbers.

Near the edge of the graveyard Laurel stopped again. No signs of life stirred the trees, but a faint hint of smoke wafted past her. Her lantern sputtered so she set it down behind a grave. She would have to move forward blindly—guided only by the faint glow of the fire now visible.

She swallowed back the knot in her throat. When had she backed down from anything? Laurel walked in a crouch, feeling her way as much as seeing. Though it housed a portion of the graveyard, she had avoided the forest most of her life except for when she was a too brave child.

The trees twisted over the land, taking advantage of their fallen comrades. A taste of the moon peeked out, but it was more hindrance than a help with its cast shadows. She stopped and knelt in turn until the fire's flames were not twenty paces off.

Laurel's breath caught and she grasped the trunk of a wide oak.

Hooded figures stood around the fire. Their chant-like song was a whisper as it found her. Half of Tenwich must have been there. She scanned the crowd, hoping and dreading to see a familiar face, but the hoods concealed their faces.

They must have known to keep their gathering secret. Whatever they were doing, someone would consider it wrong. Why else would they come out at night?

Laurel shook her head and crawled closer.

The gathering reminded her of the Harvest Festival—only the hoods differed and the nature of the dance. They swayed to the tune of the chant, making the fire their idol. The ceremony, because that's what it appeared to be, was both beautiful and strange.

One of the participants threw branches of an herb at the fire and the scent carried like winter and cookfires.

The person who had thrown the plant spoke, but Laurel couldn't understand the words. Either they were another language or too muffled to decipher. She crawled closer again, and something snapped under her knee.

She flinched and made herself small against a tree, but the people in robes didn't seem to notice. They started to move around the fire. The smoke increased, clouding the area. Laurel blinked back the stinging sensation and tried to focus on the group.

The smoke had risen, casting shapes like dragons. She wanted to reach out, to feel the smoke through her fingers. The air was thick, like it carried the ash on its fingertips. It coiled around her before dispersing above.

At some point, she had stood, but the robed figures had gone, disappeared without her witnessing them. She spread out her fingers and twirled in place. The last of the smoke moved with her.

Warmth softened her breast, and calm settled over her shoulders.

A figure moved toward her.

"Mother?"'

There was no mistaking the unbound hair and steady posture. Her mother stood before her. Laurel rushed forward, but by the time she reached where she had seen her mother in the smoke, she was gone.

A breeze like a breath on her ear raised the hair on her arms.

"Listen," it said. "Listen."

She stumbled back. It wasn't her mother's voice, but a nameless one. She must have been hearing and seeing things. She questioned the loose feeling in her chest. Shouldn't she be afraid? Running for her life? The smoke held ghosts.

With a calmness she didn't know she had, she turned back to the graveyard, back to the world where ghosts didn't exist. She didn't bother to disguise her steps and she walked numbly over fallen branches and undergrowth.

Was her mother trying to warn her? Her presence hadn't seemed like a warning but more as a welcoming. She wrapped her arms around herself, and she tripped on one of the old moss-covered headstones. She fell to her knees as she realized where she was.

This was where they had found Mrs. Boswell. Her hand fell in something warm, and she snatched it back. Blood like thick wine coated her fingers. She stared down at the small pool dumbly.

Panic, at last, seized her throat. She jumped to her feet, not bothering to inspect the area. Had the robed figures brought the blood? Had they robbed the graves? Were these people responsible for attacking her father? A scream bubbled up and she eased it down.

Her stomach churned. The smoke had enthralled her, and she had sensed nothing but good intentions from the group. Yet, someone was robbing graves, and where had the blood come from?

She hugged her arms and moved with tunnel vision through the graves. She collided with the one person she didn't need to see, Conner.

He grasped her shoulders and raised his lantern to see her. "Your face is white. You must be freezing."

"There are ghosts in the forest," she blurted out.

He chuckled. "I'm sure."

"No." She locked onto his gaze. "There are

ghosts."

"All right. I believe you." He rubbed his hands over her arms. "Let's get you home before you freeze."

"You don't understand. I saw a gathering around a fire. Ghosts came from the smoke."

His eyes widened. "That shouldn't have happened." He shook his head. "You can tell me all about it later. It's well past midnight."

"Why are you out here? How did you find me?"

"I told you I would help. Besides, it wasn't hard to find you. You made as much noise as a child in leading strings. Whatever you saw, it's gone now."

She started in place and met Conner's eyes. She tossed his hands aside. "I have to go."

Laurel bolted for home, leaving Conner to stare after her.

Chapter 9

Laurel's chest ached as she remembered the night before. She must have imagined it all. Ghosts didn't exist and why would the people of Tenwich gather around a fire? It appeared to be witchcraft, but there was no such thing as witches. Those who were burned or hung were nothing more than innocent citizens caught in the wrong web.

She was fortunate her father hadn't noticed her absence; Allie, on the other hand, had—but her sister kept it to herself. Laurel often wondered how many secrets her sister held, and why she held on to them. It was like her knowing more than she should, but she never gave a glimpse into her mind.

She didn't, however, refrain from telling Laurel what she thought.

"You need to be more careful."

"Father was asleep."

Allie pulled back a strand of blonde hair and stared at Laurel. "You know what I mean. They could have seen you, or you could have been hurt."

Laurel shrugged. "They seemed harmless enough." She hadn't given Allie the details, but again, her sister always knew. Her breath caught. "What do you know?"

Allie shook her head and the strand of hair fell out of its plait again. "It doesn't work that way. All I know is that they aren't what they seem."

Laurel snorted. "I could have told you that. They were wearing robes and dancing around a fire. How much more mysterious could they be?"

"They're witches."

"That's nonsense."

"Laurel, they are the definition of witches."

She twisted her lips down. Her sister did have a point.

"I also think you should stay away from Conner."

"You too?" Laurel sank into the kitchen chair. She peeled the last of the skin from a potato. "What is it about Conner? I have no intention of sleeping with him."

"It isn't so much Conner as it is his family."

Laurel lifted her brows in question.

"That's all I know." Allie tossed some chopped carrots into a pot of water.

"Helpful as usual," Laurel muttered.

Allie shot her a glare.

Laurel raised her hands in front of her. "Fine. I'll do what you and father say. It isn't like I seek him out. He seems to find me, but for what purpose I don't know." She did know, but she didn't want to talk to Allie about it. Conner still had feelings for her, but the child she was back then and the woman she was now were two different people.

Seeing Conner only brought up mixed emotions she didn't need. She would find some hapless man to marry, and Conner would be a distant dream—that is, if her father didn't throw her out first. She was still unsure he had meant what he said. It was better to get on with her future.

"Just so you know, I don't mind covering for you,

but please, be careful." Allie nudged her with an elbow.

They exchanged a smile.

"Thank you. I'll keep that in mind tonight." She paused. "Any idea where the blood may be from?"

Allie set down her stirring spoon and rounded on her.

"All right. All right. It doesn't work that way."

Her sister went back to stirring the pot. "You'll find someone, you know." Her voice was low, almost a whisper. "You'll love him."

"Any help finding this mysterious man? I'm assuming he is a man and not a dog." She had considered taking in a puppy.

"Laurel, get out. Find something else to occupy you. You're peeling off half the potatoes, anyway." She met Laurel's gaze. "And not the graveyard."

Laurel frowned. "Sometimes I hate you."

"I don't have to have the sight to know you plan to go there. You're my sister and you're predictable."

Laurel rolled her shoulders back and stretched. "Do you need anything from the market?"

"We could use some nice fish for dinner."

She nodded. "Fish it is."

Allie had gone back to her work and the conversation came to an abrupt end.

Laurel fetched her bonnet and gloves and set out for the market. It was a sunny day, but the air seemed to defy the brilliant rays. She shivered and increased her pace, hoping to make the market before her nose froze.

Her first stop was the bookseller. Being one of the few sources of entertainment in Tenwich, the bookseller was crowded. People from nearby cities also frequented the bookstore, and Laurel had to squeeze inside to get a glimpse of the wares.

She hadn't the funds for a book, but that didn't stop her from drooling over the titles. She was lucky if someone loaned the books she wanted to read, but would take nothing for granted and read everything that came her way. Laurel preferred adventure novels and tales of distant travels.

One such tale set in Africa caught her eye when a voice came through the murmur of the shop. It was Sally Reed, the town's too-good-for-you damsel. She spoke with her sister, Chastity, a bookshelf away.

"I don't know how she shows herself in public. Not after that display."

Chastity tut-tutted.

Laurel didn't need her sister's sight to know they talked about her. They were fully aware she could overhear them but still, Sally got louder.

"And with Conner Woodward, of all people. What could he want with her?"

What could he want with her, indeed?

Sally must have made some kind of gesture because Chastity giggled. Laurel didn't want to know. "I'm sure," Chastity added.

"He's got nothing she hasn't already had."

Laurel's face burned, and she slid toward the door. Another fine day at the booksellers. Good job, Laurel. She stepped over the threshold as an arm pushed out to open the door for her. Who better to round out her trip—Conner near collided with her on his way inside.

Laurel regarded him. "I'd advise against it unless you enjoy the Reeds."

Snickers echoed behind her.

Conner peeked over her shoulder and back to her

and nodded, but he fell into step with her. *Damnit.*

"I didn't mean for you to join me."

"Didn't you though?" A small smile twitched at the corner of his lips.

"Conner, I can't be seen with you. Go away."

He stopped mid-stride. "Oh, I see how it is. You can dance with me all festival long, but you can't have a conversation with me on the street." When he put it like that, it didn't make a lot of sense.

"It isn't you. I need to find a husband."

"Then who better than me to help." He winked. "I have the best connections in Tenwich."

Her heart did flips, and she bit down on her lip. "Why are you so dead set on helping me?" They moved out of foot traffic.

"From the way I see it, I've made your situation worse."

"Then how will this make it better?" She groaned. "I appreciate the sentiment but leave me be."

His eyes narrowed. "I guess you don't want to hear about the corpse."

"What corpse?" Her jaw slackened.

"Another corpse was taken, but not just any corpse, the last mayor."

"You're joking."

He raised a hand. "I swear I'm not."

"He's been dead for what…five years?"

"At least."

She shook her head. "What could they possibly want with a body that has been dead so long?"

He shrugged. "That's a good question. They didn't even take the whole body and the grave is a mess."

She folded her arms. "Are you doing my job for

me?"

"Your job? From what I understand, you aren't supposed to watch the graveyard."

She ground her teeth. "That doesn't mean I don't mean to."

He let out a quick laugh and sobered. "I plan to get to the bottom of this. It isn't right. Not to mention, you could get hurt."

She studied the lines of his high cheekbones and solid jaw. He meant every word of what he said, and yet....

"Why do you care?"

He stared into her eyes. The pale gray of his irises shone silver. "Besides the obvious, you know how boring life gets in Tenwich."

She wanted to kick herself for asking. Conner wasn't exactly known for his philanthropy. He maintained his father's estates and made trips to London that lasted years. He seemed to prefer the city life to Tenwich, but that only served his father's purpose. Someone had to take care of business in town.

She hadn't realized she was staring until he cleared his throat. "Sorry."

"About?"

"I'm not used to people taking an interest around here. Nobody pays me any mind."

"It's nothing."

It wasn't nothing. The last person to have a real conversation with her was Maya or Allie. Nobody took her seriously. She was the sad girl who sewed shrouds and haunted the graveyard. Her father made coffins. Who wanted to be that close to death?

Yet, it wasn't only that. She tended to push people

away before they could see her. Really see her. Laurel wasn't fascinated with death, she was in love with life, and few people understood that. Conner had once, but did he now?

It didn't matter. She wasn't supposed to be seen with him. She turned to home and bowed her head wordlessly.

He caught her arm. "You won't find the mess in the graveyard. The Reverend cleaned it up before anyone else noticed."

"He's invested in his flock, even the deceased members," she mused.

"I suspect the grave was disturbed during the Harvest Festival, even the Reverend attended." He sighed. "Everyone in Tenwich was there, but I didn't notice anything yesterday."

"Which made it the perfect time to rob graves."

"It also means nobody in Tenwich is robbing them."

She tapped a finger on her lips, forgetting where they were and who she was with. "I haven't seen anyone new here."

He gave her a small smile. "That doesn't mean there isn't someone. He could be out there, waiting for a distraction like the Festival." His gloved hand still held her arm in place, and he dropped his grip.

She frowned. "That sounds unlikely. There are plenty of graveyards throughout England. Why Tenwich? Why now? The mayor could have been dug up years ago. None of this makes any sense."

Whispers around them woke her from their conversation.

"I have to go." She turned her back to him.

"See you tonight." His words weren't a question, and they both knew she meant to investigate. How could she avoid it? How could she avoid him?

He was everywhere. He was in her thoughts, her dreams, and now he insisted on being in her life. Her father would most likely hear of their encounter at the market. If the Harvest Festival hadn't made people talk, then this surely would.

His presence was a small price to pay to find who took her mother and attacked her father. They would pay for their actions, and Laurel could settle down to the normal life her father had planned for her. Only, her life had never been normal. She wasn't sure she knew what normal was.

Without much assistance from her mother, Laurel's father had raised her and her sister as boys. He seemed to forget that boys couldn't have a trade. It had taken years for people to accept Allie's role in the business, but Laurel wasn't as lucky. She was horrible at carpentry. The more she tried to build, the more things fell apart.

If she could find these grave robbers, maybe she could prove she wasn't just a spoiled younger daughter. It was something she could do, something she was good at. She understood the graveyard the same way hunters knew the woods. Grave watching came naturally to her, and with her skill with a pistol, she was sure she had found a vocation worth pursuing.

If only she wasn't a woman.

Chapter 10

Time slowed. It moved to the point past a standstill where it seemed to move backward. The only thing that mattered to Laurel was the movement of the sun as it crawled across the sky slower than any snail. She could barely hold herself still as she waited on the edge of her bed.

She waited.

She assumed her father and sister had long since gone to bed when Laurel finally left her room. She gathered her coat and headed for the stairs. Each step was a new challenge to her patience, but she managed to land at the bottom of the stairs without breaking into a run.

She opened the door to the kitchen when her father's voice came from the parlor.

"I hope you are getting a glass of milk."

She froze in the doorway and started to back away.

"You know I can't let you run out at night. It's dangerous. Let it be."

She spun around and marched to the parlor. "How can you say that? Mother was taken."

Her father sat in the parlor with his leg propped up. His face was worn looking, as though he had rubbed it too hard, and the skin was left to hang.

Allie stood next to him, her arms folded. "We love mother as much as you do, but you're being reckless.

We'll notify a constable of what's happening."

"What can they do? Nobody knows who is responsible. If you give me a chance, I can put some holes into whoever desecrated mother's grave."

"Or they will put holes in you." Her father shook his head. "I've already lost your mother, I can't lose you too."

"It's senseless," Allie added.

"What do you expect me to do? Sit on my hands? You know I can't do that."

Her father stood from his place and the effort made him flinch. "You're going to have to learn to let other people take care of things."

"I would if they would complete them."

"Laurel, I know you don't mean that."

"What do I mean then? I'm needed out there. Who else is going to do it? You can't. The Reverend can't." They were going in circles, but her father didn't seem to hear or refused to hear what she had to say.

"I'm done having this conversation with you."

"If you would just listen."

"I've been listening." He stepped toward her and groaned. "You're not going to change my mind about this."

Allie moved to assist their father, but he shooed her away. "We'll tie you down if we have to."

Her father nodded. "Whatever it takes."

In all her years, her father had never threatened her with harm. Why was this any different? She had gone shooting alone before. Of course, she hadn't had a living target. Now wasn't the time to mention that.

"Conner can help me," she said without thinking.

Micah Atwell's face reddened. "It's you that needs

to listen. I don't want that no-good, degenerate family near mine. They've been the burnt end of Tenwich from the day they stepped into the valley. Conner is no different."

Once Laurel got her hands in something, she didn't willingly let go. "Yes, he is." She raised her chin.

"Oh, really. May I ask how you know?"

She stared forward, dumbstruck.

He nodded. "Exactly. His father will cheat and steal your clothes off your back and call it the law. He claims to own Tenwich, but he takes no responsibility for what happens here."

What her father was saying was true. From what she had gathered from the other citizens, Granger Woodward, Lord Tenwich was a selfish, uncaring man. He put people out of their homes for being pennies short on their taxes.

"Conner isn't like that."

"*Conner* is the one overseeing his interests here. Did you think of that? He put the Boswell family out on the street."

Shock jostled her heart. That couldn't be right. The Conner she had known would have helped the Boswells settle their debts, not penalize their tardiness.

The Boswells had been hard hit when the patriarch of the family died. Daniel Boswell had been a wealthy merchant who moved into Tenwich to start a family, but one misfortune after another had set the man back until he died from consumption. His widow had died shortly after, only a few short months ago.

The remaining two members lived in a ramshackle home just outside Tenwich where the Woodwards couldn't bother them. They were the first and last family everyone thought of during charitable times and prayers.

"You don't have anything to say?" Her father broke the silence.

"I just can't believe it."

"He's as ruthless and heartless as his father. The Woodwards don't have a bit of sympathy for anyone but their bank accounts. That doesn't even cover the womanizing." He spat out the words. "It isn't proper."

"Womanizing?"

He stopped as he had headed for his bed. "No. Granger and Conner have no respect for women. Neither the married nor their employees. You need to stay away from them."

An icy touch spread over her skin and seeped into her veins. No wonder her father hadn't wanted her near Conner. He was one of those men who used women and left them to fend for themselves in a world where women didn't have the luxury. Men like Granger and Conner slept with their maids and then turned them out for getting pregnant as though it was only their fault.

She shook her head, trying to banish the thoughts from her mind. What had happened to the Conner she once knew? The sweet boy who was passionate and caring. Maybe it had been an act. That boy didn't exist now or maybe ever.

"I'm sorry, father." She gave him a sad smile. "I'll stay away from the Woodwards."

He gave her a short nod. "See that you do." He left the room, leaving her with Allie.

Her sister stood in front of her, her hands clasped together, and her pale green eyes so much like Laurel's shone. "I'm sorry too, but you were being stupid."

"It's alright."

"If it means that much to you, I'll walk with you in the graveyard tomorrow."

Laurel's eyes lit up. "Would he allow it?"

"Visiting Mama's grave? Of course."

Her empty grave, but the comfort was still there, as was the graveyard. Laurel couldn't accept the offer fast enough, and she returned to her room with new hope for the following day. She couldn't watch for grave robbers, but she could monitor the graves for disturbances. Maybe if she could help in that little way, she could make a difference in catching the robbers.

She turned out the lamp on her bedside before climbing into bed. She yawned and curled into her wool blanket. It would have to be enough tonight. As much as she wanted to, she couldn't disobey her father when he stood in front of her. It was quite another thing to sneak off in the night.

A tap jostled her, but she ignored it. The autumn storms were nothing new to Tenwich.

Another tap seemed to shake the window.

She sighed and turned over, staring at the glass for answers.

Again, a tap, but this time she saw a rock bounce off the surface. What in the world?

She threw the covers off and slid to the window. Clouds overhead obstructed the moon, but a light shined too bright below. It was almost as though she read under her covers with a candle. A stupid mistake she had made as a child.

Holding the lamp was the lean figure of the last man she wanted to see.

She lit a candle so he might see her shoo him away.

He shook his head, but she flung the heavy drapes over her window and laid back down. What could that fool want? He had already given her enough trouble for a lifetime.

There. Another tap.

She groaned.

She flung the drapes aside and released the latch on the window. The glass slid open without much pressure. She raised a slipper over her head to throw at the ruffian when Conner called out.

"Wait."

"Would you keep it down?"

He moved closer until he stood just under the window. "Is that better?"

"No. It would be better if you left."

His brows pinched together in the lamplight. "Why didn't you come?"

"I have no business with you. Go away." She stepped back from the window and made to shut it.

"No, wait."

"I've told you, go away or I'll throw my shoe at you."

"Don't I deserve an explanation?"

Her eyes blazed. The Boswells could have used an explanation too. "I don't care."

He snorted and the sound seemed to travel past that of his voice. "Whatever's happened, I didn't have anything to do with it. Please, listen to me."

"You have three minutes. Then you will desist your tapping."

"The robbers were there tonight. I missed them as they were leaving. They were armed, and I was not. I wanted to be sure you hadn't run into them."

"Shouldn't my absence be answer enough?"

He shook his head. "It's a lot of ground to cover for one person. I had to be sure. As much as I know, they could have taken you with them. They carried a corpse."

Her face paled, but then a heady warmth took over. He had worried about her. They weren't even friends and he had taken the time to ensure she was safe. Guilt, like the crush of a downpour, tried her stance.

"Who was it?"

"I don't know. I couldn't tell which grave was disturbed. We'll find out in the morning."

"We won't do anything. I'll find out in the morning. You'll keep yourself to Tenwich House."

"That's the last thing I want. I'm invested in this now. You can't be rid of me."

Damnit to hell. She moved off into her room and started to pace, stopping to stare at him from the window. He folded his arms as he watched her appear and disappear. Was it his life's mission to make her life so difficult? She needed to take that walk with her sister, but she couldn't do that if he was there to intercept them.

She stared down at him. "What time?"

He dropped his crossed arms. "Nine should do it."

She nodded. "Nine it is then." Laurel and her sister would be long gone by then. She couldn't take the chance of him disturbing the ground, so they had to leave before his arrival. The only problem would be explaining to her sister why they needed to go so early when there were only a few traces of dawn.

Laurel tugged at the window, but it refused to give. She sighed.

"Why did you change your mind?"

She shrugged, wishing he would return to whatever rock was tipped over.

"You made a decision just now."

She narrowed her eyes and tugged again at the window. "More like I gave up." She groaned as the window refused to give. "Damnit."

"What did you say?" Amusement laced his voice.

"Nothing. It's this damned window."

"There it is again."

"Do shut up."

"Try wiggling it."

"I will not."

"Just do it."

Of all the stupid, idiotic ideas. She wiggled the window and it slid down a fraction. Why must he be right? She huffed out a breath.

"Don't thank me." He laughed.

She ground her teeth. "You've had your fun. Be gone."

He gave her an exaggerated bow and rose. "Get some sleep. I'll see you in the morning."

"Whatever," she mumbled to herself as she shut the window the rest of the way.

Conner skipped off as though he had accomplished some great feat. Tomorrow was one day. If he continued to insist on being involved in her investigation, she had to find some way to run him off. It would be easier if he didn't make her heart race and her palms sweat, but after what her father had revealed, her head was at least on straight.

Chapter 11

Laurel slept in patches after that. She couldn't get over the fact that Conner had been out there alone and unarmed. Was it possible that a man like him didn't own a gun? The Woodwards had always been hunters. Why was he any different?

She spent the rest of the night worrying that she was worried about him. The man had cast out the Boswells. He didn't deserve her fear or her sympathy. It wasn't until an hour before dawn that she fell asleep, and she was awakened shortly after by their self-important rooster.

She flung the covers from the bed, uncaring where they fell and dressed for the day. Black wool was the staple of her wardrobe, and she quickly donned it, preparing for a cold morning walk.

As expected, Allie had risen even before the rooster, and she busied herself in the kitchen, readying the first meal of the day.

"I thought we would get an early start," Allie said as she stirred the oatmeal.

"I thought the same."

Allie smiled at her and poured her a dish. Laurel accepted it and did what she always did, burned her mouth on the food.

"Ouch."

"Careful."

It was a daily routine, but one that didn't usually involve hunting grave robbers.

A knock sounded on the kitchen door, which could only mean one thing at this hour. Business.

Allie wiped her hands on her apron and unlatched the door.

"Sorry to disturb you this early."

"It's no bother."

"My wife passed last night."

Laurel got up to join her sister at the door. The balding man twisted his hands around his hat, his face a puffed-up version of itself. She didn't recognize him, but she didn't know everyone in Tenwich. The town was big enough that she never encountered some people.

"I'm sorry to hear that." Allie patted the man's shoulder. Laurel nodded along with her.

"Could you... "

"Yes, of course. We'll take care of everything, Mr. Harkness."

Laurel gave him a reassuring smile.

"Thank you, young lady."

She wished she had mastered her sister's empathy. Allie seemed to instinctually know what to say and do. After their mother died, Laurel knew how valuable the skill was. She had learned to keep quiet and let her sister handle things, for fear of saying all the wrong things.

The man bobbed his head as he left. A weight seemed to have lifted from the poor man's shoulders as he rushed toward the church.

"I'm sorry, Laurel. We're going to have to postpone our walk."

"Now? You're going to make it now?"

Allie sighed. "If father was feeling up to it, I wouldn't have to, but we already have more jobs than I can handle."

"I'm sorry. I had no idea."

Allie gave her a small smile. "I will manage it. Clean up the kitchen, will you?"

Laurel scrunched up her nose but agreed.

Her sister finished her breakfast with a few breaks between mouthfuls. Laurel watched with guilt gnawing at her belly and ended up not finishing her own breakfast. When Allie exited the kitchen to the workshop, Laurel cleared off the table. Her father had been scarce since he was attacked, and they didn't expect him up this early. Still, she set some of the food aside for him in case he woke in time.

She started to sweep the floor when a light tapping stopped her.

"Allie is in the workshop," she called.

The person knocked again.

She groaned and set the broom aside. "I'm sorry for your loss but Allie isn't here."

She swung open the door and Conner stood on the other side, his fist raised to knock again. "I'm not here for Allie."

"What do you want?"

"Good morning to you too."

"Conner, why are you here?"

"We were going to meet at the graveyard, but I had a better idea."

Whatever his better idea, it would prevent her from doing anything herself. Why couldn't he take a hint?

"I changed my mind." She moved to shut the door.

He rolled his eyes. "Not when you see what happened last night."

Her head swiveled to meet his gaze. "What happened?"

"You'll have to come to find out."

She folded her arms. "Just tell me. You've already said you intercepted some grave robbers."

"And that was the start." He glanced behind her, and she looked back, expecting to see her father, but there was nobody there. "Come with me." He grabbed her hand and tugged.

"Really, I must stay. I have a shroud to make."

Conner paled. "I heard, but this can't wait."

She jerked her hand away. "Fine. Will you leave me alone if I come this time?"

"I can't guarantee that. Didn't you want to find out what happened to your mother?"

Laurel bit her lip, but she stepped forward and closed the door behind her. "Listen, Conner. My father—"

"He doesn't like me or my family." He nodded.

"It isn't just that."

He met her eyes and her heart leaped into her throat.

"You don't like me either." He sighed. "It doesn't matter."

She continued to chew her lower lip. How could he be so insistent to help her when she had misgivings about him? Laurel certainly wouldn't want to help someone who didn't like her, but she did like him. Against her better judgment and everything her father had said, she still liked him.

She wanted to kick herself.

"My father can't know."

"When do I have the chance to speak to your father?"

"Nobody can know. Somebody is bound to talk. He'll find out."

"Would you rather stay here?" His brows pinched together.

"No." She started on the path to the graveyard, and he sped to catch up to her. With his long strides, he had to slow to keep pace with her.

What was she doing? This was the worst idea she had had in some time, and that was saying something. Laurel was full of bad ideas, and now she wasn't just courting her father's anger, she was flirting with her future. How many times had she told herself that Conner was bad news, that he was off-limits? And still, she was here with him, and no matter how many times her father warned her off, she was drawn right back.

A breeze caught the edge of her mahogany hair and she pushed it back into her messy bun. She tugged her shawl closer, hoping to ward off the rest of the chill, but it did nothing for the numbness that had already spread past her nose to her cheeks. What they could see of the sun did nothing for the cold. Whatever Conner wanted to show her, better be good.

The dirt mixed with dried leaves crumbled under her boots as Conner took the lead. It took her a moment to realize where he was headed, but when she did, an icy finger slid up her spine that had nothing to do with the cold.

At last, he came to a halt at the edge of the forest.

"It was right here."

"What was?"

"The doll."

"A doll." She smacked her lips. "You brought me out here for a doll."

He continued his scan of the area. "It was hanging right here." He indicated a branch.

"Well, there is no doll."

"You don't believe me."

She clicked her tongue. "Why would there be a doll at the edge of the graveyard? I've seen people put them on graves but there isn't a grave here. At least, not that I know of."

"That's just it. It wasn't a normal doll. It was made out of corn."

She blinked. "What? Are you sure you're feeling well?"

He clenched his jaw. "I'm fine."

"You don't look fine."

Purple half-moons had settled under his eyes, but somehow it made him more attractive than ever. He had spent nights watching the graveyard. Did he know how much it meant to her? Or was he just as curious as she was? She shook her head. Definitely the latter.

She placed a hand on his shoulder and jerked it back when she realized what she was doing. She cleared her throat. "You should get some rest."

"Laurel, I'm the only one watching now. Unless you plan to make a trip out tonight?"

"It isn't that easy."

He folded his arms. "You're perfectly capable of sneaking out."

"My father was waiting for me."

"What about the tree?"

She bit her lip. Of course, he would remember the

tree outside her window, but she hadn't dared to climb it since she was a young girl. The tree was larger now and probably easier to scale, but that didn't mean she wanted to fall to her death.

"That isn't happening." Even now, she was thinking of ways she could hoist herself into the tree's branches. Conner was a horrible influence on her. What if she couldn't get down or back up again?

"I know you can do it. You're stronger than you once were."

"I wasn't afraid of breaking my neck then."

"Where's the fun in staying behind?"

"Conner, if I get myself killed, I swear I'll haunt you until you die, and then I'll haunt your ghost until you're driven mad."

He waved this away. "You'll be fine."

"I can't believe I'm considering this," she mumbled to herself and brushed her wayward hair lock aside. "You brought me out here for a doll?"

He averted his gaze. "I have something for you."

He dangled a locket from his fingers, and she snatched it from his hand.

Her brows raised. "That was my mother's. Where did you find it?"

"It was a few feet from her grave. It must have fallen when they…" He cleared his throat, "you know."

She beamed. "Thank you." If they didn't locate her mother's body, at least she had this. Laurel didn't remember her mother being buried with it, but she could see Allie wanting to include it. Her mother had always worn the gold locket. It contained miniatures of her two children, which had been a present from her father when times were better.

It couldn't have come at a more fortunate time. With her father injured, they were low on wages. As fast as Allie worked, she couldn't make up for her father's income. Looking at the low gleam of the locket in the dim sunlight, she knew she couldn't sell it. The necklace had meant too much to her mother.

"You don't have to thank me. I know how much she meant to you."

"Is that why you're helping me?"

"More or less. If word gets out someone is robbing graves, Tenwich will be in chaos. My father isn't likely to restore order so it's up to me to prevent it."

She dropped her gaze. "Orderly citizens pay taxes on time."

He nodded. "You know how superstitious people are around here."

She hated to admit she was one of them. Disturbing graves meant more than just disrespect, it meant unrest. She needed to believe her mother wasn't out there alone and afraid, wandering as a lost ghost. What Laurel had seen in the woods more than unsettled her. It proved beyond her doubts that ghosts were real, but she wasn't about to admit her fears.

"Is that what you think those people were doing in the forest?"

"Superstitious nonsense, yes."

She swallowed. "And the doll?"

"More pagan practices. Tenwich is full of them."

What would he say if she admitted she believed in many of these practices? Again and again, they had proven true. How many times had she chanted over the shrouds she made? Or made a wish at the well? If she was bad, Allie was worse with her knowing ways.

He straightened his stance. "In any case, I don't know what it has to do with the grave robbers. It can't be a coincidence, but what would pagans want with bodies?"

She shook her head. "I didn't see any evidence of corpses when I saw them." She didn't know why she needed to defend the people around the fire, but she was confident that they couldn't be involved. It was the welcome sensation she had experienced in their presence.

"We need to talk to them."

"They seemed pretty secretive. I don't think they would welcome our questions."

"We still have to find them first." He caught her gaze and gave her a half-smile.

Her heart skipped and stomped as she stared.

He made a short bow and dipped his hat. "I'll see you tomorrow."

Conner sped off before she could refuse, but she had no intention of crawling down that tree. Bodies or no bodies.

Chapter 12

When the sun crested over the horizon and the rooster shouted his dominance over the land, Laurel stretched from the bed. She quickly slipped on a gray, almost black gown that settled below her breasts.

She donned her slippers, her favorite bonnet, and dressed her hair back with a few strands falling forward. Today she would call on Maya. Laurel hadn't seen her friend since the Harvest Festival, and it was past time they caught up.

Allie had already set off for the workshop, creating badly needed funds. Guilt clamped down on Laurel's heart. She didn't know how to help the family aside from finding a husband, and that was where Maya came in.

Her friend knew everything there was to know about Tenwich and many people from the surrounding areas. Maya had found several matches for herself, and she would be married if it wasn't for her picky nature.

Laurel couldn't afford to be picky, not anymore, and when she stepped over the threshold to the Meadows home, she knew she had come to the right place when voices filtered through from the parlor.

"You're right, Miss Meadows," an unfamiliar baritone said.

She rounded the corner to the parlor and stopped mid-stride. The owner of the voice was an Adonis. His sunny brown hair caught the light in such a way as though he held a halo over his head. He was broad of shoulder and strong-jawed. If the Romans had a model for their sculptures, it would be him.

Maya introduced him as Mr. George Masters, and the man's bright blue eyes seemed to ignite when he bowed to her. Her heart did a backflip, and she sat across from him beside the fire. Maya giggled at her reaction, and Laurel's face heated.

"It's a pleasure, Miss Atwell."

Her mouth dried. "Indeed?"

He had a wistful smile. "Miss Meadows has told me so much about you. She says you sew shrouds? What an excellent occupation."

"I wouldn't call it excellent, but thank you." She beamed back at him. Her shroud making made little in the way of funds, but she liked to think she was helping the community.

"I was dying to meet your acquaintance. Fortunately, you chose now to visit with your dear friend."

Why hadn't Maya told her about this man? He was the definition of perfection. She waited for the big disappointment he must drop on her.

"Mr. Masters is a solicitor. He's visiting his aunt in Tenwich."

"Indeed?"

Maya giggled. "He went to Eton with my cousin, Bertrand."

"How wonderful." Her breath caught. Every detail added to the man's significance. She would hound her friend in private and get the full details on this vision. "Will you be in Tenwich for long?"

He smiled, revealing a set of dimples. Dimples. "I'm here for the foreseeable future. My aunt wanted my help with her estate."

"Am I acquainted with her?"

Beside her, Maya nudged her. "Lady Quinn is well known to us."

Lady Quinn? Lady Quinn. His aunt was Countess Miranda Quinn? The woman hadn't left her estate in years, and though she lived in Tenwich it was on the far side of the valley, which was often forgotten. How could Maya know this man? She hadn't any connections to Lady Quinn, regardless of what she may say.

"We aren't strangers then." The confidence radiated off of him.

"Indeed?"

Maya poured Laurel a cup of tea, and she smiled at her friend in gratitude. Finally, something that would distract her from the man.

"Miss Meadows also told me you are acquainted with Mr. Woodward." He eyed her sideways.

"Not so much." She glared at her friend.

"Did you or did you not dance with him at the Harvest Festival?" Maya asked.

Was her friend matchmaking or only trying to embarrass her?

"Yes, but—"

"I feel it is my duty to warn you about that unsavory man," Mr. Masters sipped his tea.

"Your warning is noted."

"I've run into him thrice at my club. He is rather repellant."

Laurel's forehead creased, and her hands curled

into fists. "How so?"

"It is rather too gruesome for a lady's ears."

She leaned forward. "Then it is fortunate that I'm no lady."

His eyes widened. "If such a thing were true, I would have told you."

Maya frowned at him. "You're no fun, Mr. Masters. If you're going to bring up the topic of an unsavory gentleman, then I suggest you give us details or kindly let yourself out."

He chuckled. "The gossips say he's quite mad."

"Mad?"

"Mad."

"If that were the case, why doesn't his father keep him locked up?" Maya asked.

He coughed on a laugh. "He is his father's only heir. Mad or not, someone has to inherit the estate and his cousin is far worse."

"Surely something can be done."

Laurel nodded.

"Doctors across England and Europe have been consulted. They all arrive at the same conclusion. He is incurable."

"He seems to do well in society." Laurel snatched a biscuit off the table.

"He's well trained." Mr. Masters paused and looked from side to side. "Don't tell anyone I've told you this, but the man sees things."

Laurel choked on her biscuit. Maya patted her back and stared at her with concern.

"See, now I've upset you." Mr. Masters shook his head.

"Nonsense," Maya said. "We've heard worse.

Haven't we, Miss Atwell?"

Laurel frowned. She didn't know what her friend was referring to, but she nodded along with her anyway. Maya had a habit of stretching the truth. It made for colorful conversation, but it also made it difficult to tell what was factual. She hoped Mr. Masters was the same way.

"But you haven't heard the worst part." Mr. Masters brows climbed his flawless forehead. "He communicates with the dead."

Laurel shifted in her seat when Mr. Masters made his excuses and left the parlor, promising to call on Laurel the following day. She was left with Maya and Maya's ever silent married sister, Clarissa.

Maya's sister was once a friend to Laurel, but after she had married, the new Mrs. Hampton was leagues away, physically and metaphorically. Clarissa sat now embroidering baby clothes for the child she awaited, and she had shown little interest in the presence of Mr. Masters until now.

"Quite a character." Clarissa didn't look up from her work.

"I can assure you, dear sister, Mr. Masters is normal."

Clarissa shook her head. "I mean Mr. Woodward."

"He isn't all bad," Laurel interjected.

Clarissa threw her a glance. "I have heard worse about things people do in private. At least Mr. Woodward doesn't hide behind his name. It's a shame so many of our betters are really not so."

Laurel nodded. "Who's to say any of it is true?" She swallowed to keep back any revealing words.

Maya snorted. "Laurel, just because you're in love

with him, doesn't mean he's not mad."

Clarissa raised a brow.

"I am not in love with him."

Maya mimicked her sister's expression.

"I'm not."

"He's all you talk about these days."

"I swear the man is stalking me. That doesn't mean I'm in love with him. He's been helpful looking for grave robbers."

Maya pursed her lips. "You haven't found a single graverobber. What do you do at night?"

Laurel bit her lip. "It isn't that easy."

Maya and Clarissa shared a smile.

She stood and turned on her friend. "I don't have to take any more of your abuse today."

Maya waved a hand. "Sit down. I'm only teasing."

Laurel dropped back down next to Maya. She couldn't seem to decide what to do with her hands. At last, she settled for smoothing her skirts. Of course, her friend saw right through her dilemma and gave her a pointed look. Laurel glared back at her, and Maya didn't comment on it.

"Love, or not, I, for one, find him exciting." Maya smiled. "Seances are becoming quite the thing in some circles."

Clarissa nodded. "He is most interesting."

"Maya, you wouldn't survive a seance. You can't even kill a spider."

Maya pointed a finger at her. "Ghosts are different. Last I heard, they don't bite you."

Laurel laughed. "I wouldn't be so sure. From what I understand, ghosts do all sorts of damage. Some people even claim ghosts possess them and make them do terrible things like murder their spouses."

"That's nonsense. Those people are mad. Ghosts are as harmless as every other person you meet."

"I wouldn't say that's harmless."

"My point is that ghosts are individuals like people. Most are innocent and not prone to violence. Sure, there will be some unsavory ones, but the majority are good."

Laurel blinked. "Maya, you certainly have a high opinion of people. I thought you had experienced more of society."

"Exactly so."

Laurel shook her head. "I disagree. I don't think people are good deep down as you're implying."

Maya dropped her arm over Laurel's shoulders and squeezed. "You haven't met the right people, my dear. Don't worry. I will remedy that. Mr. Masters isn't the only suitable gentleman for you."

"Mr. Masters is far above my station. I might as well shoot for an earl or a duke. Maybe the crown prince of France."

"That's the spirit."

Laurel gawked.

"Don't sell yourself short," Clarissa said as she side-eyed Laurel. "Mr. Masters may be your superior but that doesn't mean you don't hold any appeal. Have you looked in the mirror lately? You've grown into a beautiful young woman."

Laurel glanced away. "It doesn't matter if I'm attractive. I have no dowry to speak of, and my father is the cabinetmaker. What could a man like Mr. Masters want with me?" She didn't argue about Clarissa's assessment of her, but she knew she wasn't any better than plain. She was built small with lackluster brown hair and dull green eyes that were missing the spark Allie's eyes had.

If Mr. Masters couldn't want anything from her, then Mr. Woodward certainly didn't care for her. What was she doing with him? A relationship with him was impossible, and she wasn't like Maya. She wouldn't sleep with anyone before marriage, and Mr. Woodward was far superior to Mr. Masters, regardless of what society said.

Lord Granger Woodward was a baron and Conner was his heir. A future titled man was not someone Laurel should be swooning over. Mr. Masters seemed far more obtainable in comparison. It didn't help Conner had lied to her.

"Mr. Masters will call on you, I promise." Maya winked. "Then you can tell me all about the children you will have."

Laurel rolled her eyes. "I wouldn't go that far."

"Oh really? Remind me who Florence and Edgar are?"

She averted her gaze.

"Who are they?" Clarissa asked.

"Only Laurel's children with Mr. Woodward."

"Stop. That was years ago. I was a different person." She bit her lip and looked away.

Maya slapped her hand. "I've known you since we were in leading strings. You haven't changed since the day we met. I'd imagine the names may have changed but you still dream about your future with him."

Laurel sucked in a breath. Her friend wasn't wrong, but her musings were harmless. Nobody but Maya, and now Clarissa, knew about her pining. It wasn't as if she was going to declare her love for the man. It was an innocent interest that she had no intention of acting on. Maya simply could not believe Laurel wouldn't sleep with him.

She got to her feet. "I'm afraid I have more chores to take care of today."

"Chores can wait." Maya frowned.

"And have Allie hound after me? No, thank you. I'll see you tomorrow?"

Maya nodded, but her attention was already elsewhere when she picked up a book from a side table. Laurel would have been offended if it had been anyone else but her dearest friend. Maya was addicted to novels and had little interest in human interaction when she had found a good one. It was a wonder she kept up socially.

Laurel pulled on her coat and bonnet and let herself out. It was uncharacteristically warm that October day, and she regretted not bringing a lighter coat. Still, it was only a ten-minute walk from the Meadow's house to the Atwell's house. She had to make her way through the town center on her way to the edge of town where she lived.

She crossed her fingers as she went, hoping she wouldn't run into anyone she knew on the way. She had already spent too much time at Maya's, and Allie needed all the help she could get. Maya would argue that Laurel was husband-hunting, but Laurel knew the truth, Mr. Masters was humoring her, nothing more.

Laurel dodged a pile of horse dung in the road and collided with a male chest. Instead of the man's identity being the one of her dreams, such as in a romance novel, the eldest Boswell son, Randal, stood attached to the chest. He was a little older than Laurel and yet he had the maturity of a teenager.

"Excuse me," Laurel said, putting distance between them.

He waved a hand, and a whiff of alcohol met her nostrils. "Think nothing of it." He belched and blinked. "Oh, Laurel, funny seeing you here."

Her face hardened. "It's Miss Atwell, and what is so odd about me being here?" She frequented the town center on market days and the local bookseller knew her by name. She couldn't imagine what he was referring to.

"I didn't think you would show your face after that public display of whoring Mr. Woodward."

"It was a dance."

He snorted. "Indeed, and you enjoyed yourself, didn't you?"

She clenched her hands into fists. "I don't have time for this nonsense."

He raised his brows. "Too busy sneaking around, I take it. Don't mind me."

The color drained from her face. "What do you mean?"

He wiped a hand over his runny nose, adding to the redness of his face. "You know what I mean. What would dear Mr. Atwell say if he knew his youngest daughter snuck out at night to be with that loathsome blackguard?"

She opened her mouth, but no words came.

"That's right. I've seen you sneak off with him. Him in his tailored suits from Town. Did you know one of those suits could feed my family for a year?"

Laurel sucked in a breath. "I'm sorry, Mr. Boswell."

"Sorry?" His jaw set. "Sorry doesn't put food on my table or bring my poor mother back. Sorry is for those that can afford to live another day, while my family scrapes by on charity and root vegetables. You, of all people, should know what it's like."

She blinked. "How do you mean?"

He sniffed. "That's right. You're sheltered from the worst of your father's finances. It wasn't just that injury that took funds out of him."

Her heart froze a beat. "How do you know this?"

"The man has to get it off his chest."

Laurel shook her head. "I don't believe it. He wouldn't talk to you."

He grunted. "You're right. He wouldn't, but he confided in the Reverend."

Her brows drew together. "What were you doing listening in on a private conversation at church? Have you no decency?" The man wasn't fit to kiss her father's boot and certainly not fit to hold her father's secrets. What a mess Mr. Boswell had made.

"You listen here. I wasn't eavesdropping. Not on purpose. I woke up in church, and they were talking. Couldn't even give me a decent sleep."

She pinched the bridge of her nose. "What were you doing sleeping in the church?"

"It's warmer than the ground."

She huffed out a breath. She couldn't fault him for needing a place to sleep. The Boswells were decent people and at least that was what she was led to believe. She questioned whether Randal was from the same line, but of course, the drunk wasn't talking sense.

She laid a hand on his shoulder. "Why don't you sleep this off?"

"I'm not drunk, and I'm not a fool." He paused. "I say this because I care about your family. Your sister has helped me through hard times. You should think twice before aligning yourself with Mr. Woodward. He's a scoundrel. He'll cheat your father the same way he cheated me. You look down on me now but wait until you fall as hard, if not harder."

He gathered his coat about him and left with a finesse she would have laughed at if there was any room in her heart for laughter. Although Randal was a broken man, he made sense. She didn't doubt he told the truth.

Why hadn't her father told her they were having so much trouble? He must have confided in Allie, or her sister wouldn't be working nonstop. She supposed he had told her in a way. Marry, he had said. He didn't want or need the burden of her anymore.

A weight pressed on her shoulders and chest. If she was going to pull herself and her family out of this, she needed to marry. She already knew it was where she was headed, and yet, she hadn't realized the seriousness of the situation. What would happen if their money ran out? Would they be on the streets with the Boswells? Scrambling for charity and sleeping on the church pews?

The more she thought about it, the more Mr. Masters seemed like a possibility. Why not her? She would make a good wife though an eccentric one. She would gladly give up her romantic musings in the graveyard and shroud sewing to save her family.

Her chest dropped. She would have to give up finding her mother and holding those accountable for their crimes against the dead. A married woman didn't play detective any more than she roamed the graves, but for now, she wasn't married yet.

Chapter 13

Later that night, her heart was in her throat as she pulled herself onto the tree branch. Her fingers dug into the rough bark of the tree, and the world swayed when she glanced down. She gritted her teeth as though keeping her head steady would prevent her from falling.

"That's it," Conner said from below.

"I told you, I don't need your help."

"Does this look like I'm helping?"

She swung her leg over the branch and carefully scooted toward the trunk, tugging at her skirts after the fabric snagged on the bark. A flush crept up her cheeks as she imagined how she must look like from below.

Her foot found a hold in the center of the branches, and she continued down.

"I don't know what you were afraid of. You're doing great."

She spun, finger raised to answer him, and her other grip slid from under her fingers. She made a frantic attempt to steady herself, but instead, she tilted down, and the grassy floor came to meet her.

Laurel landed hard on her back, but managed to roll to her side just in time to spare her head from the impact. Her nerves became lightning rods, every muscle jolted by the fall. Her hands burned from the mad grasp at the last second. She had snuck out against her better judgment, but she needed answers from

Conner, no matter the risk.

"I told you not to let go." Conner stood over her, shaking his head.

She scowled. "You told me a lot of things."

"Then you were listening?"

"No, but your voice distracted my thinking."

He leaned down and caught her right hand. She winced.

"This needs to be sewn up." He indicated a deep cut along her palm.

"I'm sure it's fine." She rolled to her knees and set herself back on her feet. She wobbled for a moment but caught her balance on the tree.

"It isn't fine. You're bleeding. Not to mention the bruises you likely acquired."

She ground her teeth. "What do you want me to do? I can't go back inside like this."

"Well, you can't go to the graveyard with this cut. It will get infected."

She folded her arms, winced, and slowly unfolded them. "What do you have in mind? I can't see anyone in Tenwich. There will be talk." Nobody needed to know she had fallen from a tree outside her window. Young women only climbed out of their windows for one thing, and she would rather not be associated with Conner's name in that regard.

"We'll go to Tenwich House. I have everything we need."

She wasn't sure how that was any better, but the idea sparked her curiosity. "If you insist, but you owe me answers."

The little girl inside Laurel wanted to jump up and down. She had never visited Tenwich House, and yet, it had been a constant structure looming over her life. It was the one building she had never had reason to access, which had driven her quite mad as a child.

Conner studied her. "Can you walk?"

She smiled and took a step. The ground seemed to heave to and fro, but her legs adapted to the strange perception. She took another step to prove her point and teetered to the side.

Conner grunted and shoved an arm under her shoulders. Her cheeks colored and she hid her face in his chest. When the scent of spice overwhelmed her, her face blazed, realizing what she had done, and she jerked away from him. He refused to lose his grip on her and steadied her back toward him.

"This is ridiculous. What if someone sees?"

"Then we'll have to tell them the truth, but nobody is going to be out at this hour. Besides, it's too dark." He lifted his lamp from off the ground, but it made little progress in the darkness.

Tenwich House was on the other side of town. They would have to traverse past the other homes to reach it.

She mumbled a prayer as they ambled over the road. No lights came from beyond the windows, but that didn't mean nobody watched. She shifted in his hold, wishing she had brought something to cover her face. Still, she kept her face tilted away from the lamp and relied on Conner's guidance to find the way.

"A little help?" He stopped in the center of the road.

"I'm sorry." She adjusted her weight. "Is that better?"

His lip twisted up. "I suppose."

"Look, I can't make this any easier unless you let go of me." She scanned the houses for any sign of life.

"We'll do fine." He took back up their march.

The ground was uneven where wagon wheels had fallen during the last storm, but they pressed on, navigating the rough patches until Tenwich House came into view. It sat in the distance on its proud hill, but tonight, it was only a shadow against the starry night sky.

A shape moved to her left, away from Conner.

"Did you see that?"

"See what?"

The shape moved again out of the corner of her eyes. "There." She nodded toward the offending movement.

"I don't see anything. Maybe it's a dog."

She snorted. "Dog my foot. It was bigger than a dog. You're sure nobody is out here?"

They paused, and he released her. She shivered as his warmth left with him.

"Why would anyone be out here? Even the grave robbers have more sense than to walk the streets without a light. How do you think I found them that night?" He pointed to his own lamp.

"Right."

"We're almost there." He walked off, leaving her to fend for herself.

She grumbled but kept her feet.

The surrounding space darkened the closer they got to Tenwich House. Conner didn't seem to know the difference, but Laurel slowed her pace, forcing him to do likewise. The autumn breeze died as they sought the shelter of the building. The dirt road turned to large, flat stones.

Guarding the entrance, the statue of a man in the fountain appeared as though it would sound an alarm at any moment as it raised a horn to the sky. Gooseflesh raced across her arms, and she rubbed her skin.

Laurel couldn't help but wonder what Lord Tenwich would think of her presence. She tried to mimic Conner's unconcern, but instead, ended up grasping her injured hand to her chest and staring at shadows.

She winced as Conner led them directly to the front door. The heavy wood made no sound as it glided shut behind them. The expanse before them took on qualities of a cave. She imagined if she stepped out of place, she would fall into a pit on the floor. She followed close behind Conner, and his lamp did little to ease her imaginings.

Conner turned onto a broad staircase that dominated the shadowy space. Her sense of depth had gone with the light. Yet, the stairs went on. Their carpeted length seemed to push back against her boots.

At last, Conner stopped at a new floor. Without hesitation, he swung left.

Laurel let out a squeak and hurried to catch up. She kept her gaze on his advancing steps and neglected to realize when he halted. Her head found his back, and he grunted and pulled her up beside him.

The door Conner unlocked was like the other doors in the hallway. A solid, unmarked barrier lined by portraits of dead ancestors who stared at her in defiance. She leveled her gaze on Conner's back and followed him into the room.

Inside, a fire glowed low, forcing her to examine

the contents of the room. A bulky four-poster bed stood proudly in the center of the room. A desk sat off to the far side, grouped with an armoire and a chest. Windows lined the opposite wall, covered with heavy drapes in a color she couldn't quite name. They were neither blue nor green, but almost black.

Without a word, Conner opened the armoire and took out a sewing kit. He pointed to the chair at the desk. "Sit here."

She complied, marveling at the comfort of the wood beneath her.

He lifted his lamp again and disappeared out the same door they had entered from.

Laurel was left with a gnawing sense to flee the room. What would her father think if he knew she was in Conner's bedroom, of all places? Allie certainly would gawk at her stupidity, but she couldn't think of another way to appease the man than allow him to treat her cut.

Moments passed and she wondered if Conner had forgotten her. When he finally appeared, it was as though he had materialized from the air. He removed the bowl of water from a side table and placed it under her hand on the desk.

She sucked in a breath as he washed the wound, seeing the deep gash for the first time.

He poured a strong scented liquid over her hand, and light slammed into the back of her eyes.

"What is that?" she yelped.

He shook his head. "Alcohol."

He took the sewing kit and proceeded to thread a needle before he attacked her hand.

"Do you know what you're doing?"

112

His crooked smile told her enough.

"At least, don't let it scar."

"There isn't much helping that."

Her head grew woozy, and she almost forgot Conner stood over her, his hands clasped around her own. Her heart slammed into her chest. The spice and cedar scent of him added to her buzzing head.

She took in a long breath as she examined his lopsided work. "At least it is closed."

"You're welcome."

"All the same." She scrambled to her feet, but stood too quickly and collided against Conner's chest.

"This is becoming a habit of yours." Amusement pinched his eyes. "Sit down."

He pulled a green bottle from his coat and grabbed a small glass from the side table. Conner poured a healthy gulp of green liquid. She examined the contents and sniffed. The scent didn't slam into her senses the way the alcohol had, but even so, it jostled her.

She sipped and a licorice-like flavor stung at her tongue. She downed the rest without a second thought, knowing if Conner wanted her dead, he wouldn't have bothered to sew up her hand.

He patted her on the back and stepped to the side. "You'll feel better soon."

She snorted. "I felt well before."

"You weren't even walking straight."

Laurel scrunched up her nose. "I was walking just fine."

He frowned. "It's getting late. We don't have time to patrol the graveyard tonight."

She blinked at the windows, which gave nothing away. "How can you know what time it is? I'm sure we have enough to make a circuit of the graves."

"It's nearly three. There's a clock on the mantel."

"Oh." She examined her hand as the air between them buzzed.

"Let me take you home."

She moved without protest and found herself with her arm woven into his. She couldn't seem to go without touching him, but at the same time, she couldn't undo their connection for fear of offending him.

Laurel followed him once more through the house, but this time she took no notice of her surroundings. The thrill of seeing Tenwich House had disappeared when reality sat around her. It was an old, unforgiving structure, and she would rather not explore its dark corners.

The breeze had taken on a new sense of urgency, and the chill numbed her face all at once. The stars had made an appearance, and she found herself entranced by their defiance of the house they exited.

Her gaze dropped to the road and a figure walked the dirt path toward them.

"Who is that?" She squinted at the silhouette.

Conner was silent for a moment. "Who?"

"The man in the road."

"I don't see anyone. Maybe the absinthe is playing tricks on you."

"Absinthe? You gave me absinthe?"

"What did you think it was? There's nothing better for the swelling."

She groaned. "Now I'm seeing things."

"What does he look like?"

"Who?" She rubbed a hand over her face.

"The man in the road."

"Well, he looks like…the old mayor. That can't be right."

"Laurel, you're seeing a ghost."

She slowed her pace. "No, I'm not. It's my imagination."

"Then explain the apparition in the road."

She halted in place and planted her fists on her hips. "You said you couldn't see him."

He combed a hand through his locks. "It doesn't matter if I can or can't see the ghost. It matters that you can." He grasped her shoulders and steadied her. "Don't you see what this means? You saw your mother last night."

"That's impossible."

Conner's gray gaze darkened. "I assure you, it's not."

She huffed. "Then why am I seeing them now? Why haven't I seen them before?"

"For one thing, the absinthe probably helped."

"I didn't have absinthe before. How do you explain me seeing my mother?"

He shook his head. "I don't know. Maybe something the pagans were burning."

This couldn't be right. Conner was teasing her. The absinthe must be making her see things. And her mother? She saw what she wanted to see. It was only wishful thinking that led her to see these things, nothing more.

"If you're telling the truth, why is it you can see them without aid? None of this makes any sense."

"I can't explain it. I've never needed any help."

"Then why do you spend time in the graveyard? I'd

imagine it must be uncomfortable to spend time with ghosts."

He chuckled. "You would be surprised how few ghosts are in the graveyard. Most of them roam where they lived or died. They have little connection to the ground they are buried."

"All right, say I believe you. What is my mother doing in the forest?"

"I guess that she was looking for you. Either that or she has some connection with the pagans."

Her jaw dropped. "My mother was a church-going woman. What use would she have for their rituals?"

"You might not know your mother as well as you thought you did."

Her green eyes took on a fierce glare. "How do I know you aren't lying to me? What else are you keeping from me? Do you know what happened to the bodies?"

He sighed. "I know as much as you do."

"You lied about seeing ghosts. How can I believe you? Believe anything you say?"

"It didn't come up."

Her brows scrunched together. "At what point in time is it appropriate to ask someone if they can see ghosts? Why didn't you tell me when I first saw my mother?"

"I wasn't sure you did see her."

She gestured her hands upward, wincing as pain flared in her injured hand. "Conner, I don't know what to think. Why am I seeing ghosts?"

He studied her as they lapsed into silence. He appeared to struggle with what he would say next. "Laurel, you're sensitive."

"What does that mean?" Her voice came out in a roar.

"You can see ghosts. You just need a little help."

"I don't want a little help. I want to not see them. Don't you understand?"

He lifted a hand, palm up. "I don't, actually."

Her hardened jaw softened, and she let the words die between them. His face was worn and the purple crescents under his eyes seemed to have deepened. Of course, he was tired. He hadn't slept for days in her estimation. How did one sleep when they could see ghosts?

"You must get tired of it."

A sad smile tilted his lips. "I don't, actually."

Her eyes widened. "How?"

"I don't know any different."

The admission struck her in the chest. What would it be like to see ghosts everywhere? She couldn't imagine the lack of privacy. Good God, had anyone been watching when she touched herself at night? Or heard her talking to herself when she brushed her hair?

Her cheeks blazed against the cold air, and she watched her breath cloud the space beside her.

"I have so many questions."

"Naturally, and I will answer them, but it's getting too late. Let me help you to the tree." He walked off without seeing if she would follow, and their conversation seemed to stay where they left it back on the road.

He hoisted her up into the tree, but she was too distracted to appreciate the well-formed muscles in his arms. Well, almost. How did an aristocrat stay so fit? He must do more than sign papers and kick people out of their homes.

She bit her lip and clamped onto a branch. "Is that why you decided to help me? When I saw my mother?"

He nodded. "That's part of it. I wanted to know how much you knew, what you saw. I've never met anyone else like us."

Like us. The words sent a tingle down her spine.

Laurel, you idiot. He's the last man you should want to be joined with.

Yet, there it was. The tingle had settled between her legs.

She averted her gaze and tried for the branch nearest her window. Her foot slipped, but she managed to regain her grip. "Tell me something—why were you in the crypt that day?"

Conner was silent, and she craned her head back to see, but he was no longer there.

"So much for making sure I get back safely."

She pulled her remaining foot into the window and let out a deep breath. This time she hadn't hurt herself, but what would she do about tomorrow? Did she want to pursue this with Conner? He admitted lying to her, but that didn't mean he wasn't still being untruthful.

Ghosts. She shook her head. How ridiculous. In all her twenty-one years, she had never seen the like, but would she have recognized a ghost for what it was? The whole idea was madness. She wouldn't succumb to this.

Conner had played with her mind for the last time. She would find a way to investigate the graveyard without his help, but how to avoid him. He seemed to be everywhere she wanted to be. Her attraction to him didn't help her cause either. How could her body be so blind?

She closed the window and pulled the drapes closed. She lit a candle after her eyes adjusted to the lack of light and placed it on her bedside. Her nightgown came next, but her body ached, and she decided to sleep in her clothes.

Once she settled into bed, she was startled as a paw tugged at her blanket.

Rollo. She peered down and the dog wagged his tail. Except Rollo had died two years ago. Tears stung her eyes as she studied the translucent form of the dog she had loved since childhood. His fur appeared clean, unlike the dog she knew, but he was otherwise the same chestnut-colored terrier.

She dangled a hand over the bed, and he licked her fingers. "I've missed you."

She smiled through her tears. "Well, come join me."

The ghost hopped onto the bed and curled into a ball between her knees. If she was going to delude herself, she might as well enjoy it. This absinthe was strong stuff.

Chapter 14

The next night, wind whipped her hair around her face, and she sputtered to keep going. For once, the moon made a difference in her visibility, and she managed to descend the tree with little difficulty. It was fortunate that tonight the moonlight would aid her since it was unlikely a lamp would stay lit in this wind. Still, she fetched a lamp earlier in the night from the shed off the kitchen and left it for her to find below the tree.

To her relief, Conner wasn't waiting for her at the bottom of the trunk. It was curious the man hadn't come after all the effort he had put into helping her, and she assumed she would meet him at the graveyard.

Her shoulders tightened and she pushed them back. Laurel could do this without him or her father. The grave robbers hadn't a chance against her pistol. Still, she took her steps with care, making as little sound as possible. Each crunch under her boot heightened her senses, resulting in an over vigilance.

She shielded the lamp with her hand and body, making it almost unnecessary. Her steps trudged the well-traveled path from her home to the graveyard. The field was lifeless, aside from the undergrowth that threatened to spread to the Atwell yard. In all her life, she had never seen a creature larger than a mouse move in the brush.

The graveyard came upon her as if it had waited

for her arrival. Each gravestone seemed to reflect another greeting from beyond life. She nodded to the familiar names and smiled at the mourners' flowers. It was as though she had never left, like visiting an old friend after weeks away.

A globe of light bounced deep inside the graveyard. She quickened her pace, mindful of the noise, but the wind raged through the surrounding trees, and she doubted anyone present would hear her. A shape accompanied the globes.

The shape froze, and she dashed her lamp behind a gravestone, but it was too late. He had spotted her light the same way she had seen his. She crouched, her skirts straining against the movement.

He turned away from her and set an unmatchable pace.

Laurel rose and aimed her pistol. "Stop right there," she shouted.

The man bolted as if a fire was beneath him.

"I'm warning you." She fired and the pistol gave a satisfying kick, but he had moved too far off. "Blast."

Laurel tucked the pistol away and charged after him. He was headed toward the forest. The place all secrets seemed to hide. She bounded past gravestones and over the uneven ground. When she reached the trees, the man was clear, and she dropped down on the nearest felled log.

She panted, chasing her breath.

"I almost had him."

"You were as close as a fish is to flying."

She startled, and her hand went to her breast. "Don't do that."

Conner stepped in front of her, arms folded. "What

were you thinking coming out here alone, again?"

She tossed him a small smile. "I'm not alone. You're here."

He shook his head. "How do you know he wasn't armed?"

Laurel tilted her head down and stared at him through her lashes. "He didn't shoot at me, that was enough. It doesn't matter now, anyway. Where were you?" She didn't know why she cared, but the man had grown on her.

"This isn't about me. You shouldn't even be out here to begin with."

"Don't start this again."

"Do you know how scared I was?" His hands shook in the low light. "You could have been killed."

Her heart kicked up. "Oh, do you mean you would miss me?"

"I don't need another body on my hands. We already have one."

Well, that wasn't very romantic, but since when did she need romance? *Get it together, Laurel.*

"He left the body?"

She hadn't seen him carry anything of that size, but she thought she had scared him away before he had completed his task.

"No, the man died shortly before I came to find you after that stupid shot you took. Why do you think I wasn't waiting for you?"

"I don't know. I thought maybe I had grown some new luck."

His jaw hardened.

"Who was it?" She licked her dry lips, but the dry air made quick work of them.

"Mr. Boswell."

"Randal?" Her stomach twisted.

He nodded.

"What was he doing here?" As much as she disliked the man, he didn't deserve to be murdered. He was a drunken fool, but he was a kind-hearted one.

"Probably the same thing we were, but he was drunk out of his senses. I can't imagine what he was thinking when the man killed him." He let out a breath. "That could have been you."

Her heart skipped and she laid a hand on his arm. "It wasn't."

He cleared his throat. "We need to rethink this whole operation. It's hard enough having you scale that tree, but what if you get shot? Or worse?"

She didn't ask what could be worse.

"He wasn't armed. At least, not with guns."

"Tonight, he wasn't. He was set on whatever strange course he was on. I'm surprised he didn't take Mr. Boswell with him. Your dad got lucky."

She tucked her hair behind her ears. "I don't understand him. His choices. The corpses are neither all fresh nor old. He doesn't discriminate gender or class. What could he possibly want with these bodies?"

"You're asking the wrong person." He sighed. "Come help me with the body. I don't want people to come across it in the morning. He gave me quite a scare myself."

"What about my delicate female sensibilities?"

Conner gave a deep-throated laugh, throwing his head back.

She grinned and shrugged. "It was worth trying."

He wiped tears from his eyes. "Was it?"

"I'll answer that when I see the body."

Laurel trailed after him as they moved through the graveyard and stopped just feet from the rest of the churchyard. Mr. Boswell was laid out on the path. She shook her head. Any member of his family could find him like that. Conner had chosen the best course of action.

The state of his body was another concern. Randal was beaten, presumably with a shovel, until he was unrecognizable. If it wasn't for his worn brown suit she had seen earlier, she would never have guessed his identity.

"Grab the legs."

She bent down. "Where are we taking him?"

"My first thought was your house, but I don't know how we would explain this. The next best choice would be the Vicarage."

"We would have to wake the Reverend."

He didn't reply. Instead, he hoisted the dead man from his shoulders. Laurel took her cue and lifted him by the legs. Randal's body weight seemed to grow as they carried him over the path to the Vicarage.

The Vicar's home was a welcoming stone structure built in soft lines and rounded edges. It sat minutes from the church with only a few mature trees and a lawn between them. They set the corpse down at the side of the entrance.

Conner faced her. "You should go. If there is any chance the Vicar gets word back to your father… "

"Right." She shifted in place but didn't turn to leave. "You'll let me know what happens?"

"When have I not?"

"Really? I just don't like to be kept out of things."

Her father and sister did that enough.

She stepped away.

He grabbed her arm. "Wait. Don't go out alone again."

She shrugged off his hand. "I did fine tonight."

He gave her a level look.

"All right, fine. I'll wait for you, but you better not have all the fun."

Conner snorted, but his eyes smiled back at her. He aimed a kick at her backside, and she trotted away, laughing. She hurried out of earshot, dodging into the graveyard as Conner knocked at the Vicarage. She didn't hear the reply as she put distance between them.

Someone was set on claiming these bodies, but if it was any random body, they would have taken Mr. Boswell. If she didn't find a connection between the bodies, there would be no way to prevent future robbers. So far, their watch hadn't prevented theft to her knowledge aside from tonight.

Worse, the robber was now a murderer and had almost killed her father. Maybe he would decide the cost of the corpses was too high and quit. They could only hope, but what would that mean for the corpses already taken? Where was her mother?

Conner seemed as insistent as she was to find out what was happening, but she couldn't understand why. His reasons made little sense to her reasoning, and he certainly didn't want to catch grave robbers because of her. Her heart stomped in frustration. She shouldn't even think of him in that way.

She shook her head as she neared the edge of the graveyard. The cold had died down and her heavy garments now seemed too warm.

Maybe Maya was right. Perhaps if she slept with Conner, she would no longer desire him.

She froze. Why was she even thinking on such terms? What would her father think?

Of course, her father didn't have to know. Nobody had to know. They had gotten away with sneaking out at night for innocent reasons, and Mr. Boswell may not be the only one who had seen them. Why take the blame for something she didn't do when she could enjoy herself for the same accusations?

She sighed. She was only fooling herself. Conner didn't want her. He still saw her as the young girl he had joked with. Their kiss, her first, was such a distant memory that she wondered if it had been a dream.

Laurel kicked up dirt in the path leading to her house. She certainly felt like a child. Her father wouldn't let her make her own decisions, and her sister cared for her the way she would if she had children. The only one who seemed to think she was old enough was Maya, but her friend was as young as she was.

She stared up at the tree leading to her window. The tree loomed over her like an ogre from one of the fairy tales she had read as a child. She had no desire to go back to her room, and she found herself walking away from her house.

After tonight's events, she wouldn't be able to sleep. A man was dead, and the grave robbers had gotten away. If she had arrived sooner, she might have prevented all of this trouble. Instead, it had been Conner who had found Mr. Boswell.

Conner had more success than she did as a watcher.

A chill ran up her spine. No, Conner couldn't. She

knew him, or she thought she did. What would Conner want with bodies? Did it have something to do with this madness Mr. Masters had mentioned?

What was she thinking? This was Conner. Her Conner. The man she had dreamed of having children with since childhood.

She raced back home, not bothering to duck into the shadows when she saw a shape in the distance, which turned out to be a large, black dog.

The tree no longer seemed imposing, and she scaled it in half the time. She removed her gown and dropped onto her bed.

Conner wasn't mad. She had seen the ghosts herself, hadn't she? Or maybe it had been a trick of the absinthe. Just because he could see ghosts didn't make him mad, or did the act of seeing ghosts create madness?

She tensed. Would she go mad as well?

Whatever the case, she had to be sure Conner wasn't stealing bodies with a partner. As far as she knew, he didn't have friends, but he could have hired out help. He had the funds to buy someone's silence.

She shivered. What had he been doing in the crypt that day, and why didn't he want her to know?

Her mind traveled around until she drove herself senseless and drifted off to a deep sleep. Only the gut-wrenching scream that filled the house that morning could wake her.

Chapter 15

Laurel rushed down the stairs in a blind fog. She took the stairs two at a time and rounded the banister. She didn't stop to catch her breath until Allie was in view in the kitchen. Her sister's face was pale, and her eyes were wide. She held a hand to her throat.

Laurel panted. "What happened?" She folded her arms over her nightgown when she was assured of her sister's wellbeing.

"A dog. The biggest one I've ever seen." Allie pointed at the window above the cabinets.

Laurel stepped beside her, but nothing appeared in the field leading to the graveyard. She shook her head.

"It was there."

"Allie, I believe you. I saw a dog the other day. A big, black mongrel."

Allie nodded in a quick burst. "Its eyes were a ruddy brown, almost red."

"I didn't see its eyes." Laurel glanced back at the window. "Whatever it is, it's gone now."

"You know what this means, don't you?"

"Nobody is going to die. We've had enough death to last us for a while."

Allie turned on her. "It doesn't work that way. If anything, death occurs in groups."

"It was just a dog."

"What dog?" Mr. Atwell limped into the room and

settled at the table.

"Allie saw a big dog in the yard."

"Is that what you were screaming about?"

"It wasn't just a big dog. It was a monster. Someone should put that animal down before it hurts one of the children in the neighborhood."

Laurel glared at her sister. "Just because it's big doesn't mean it's violent."

"You said you saw the dog. That one is most definitely dangerous. It snarled at me."

"You girls stay inside and keep the door shut. I don't want another dog in the house, especially not a large one. I'm going to be in the workshop." He left, shaking his head.

"If you're that worried, I'll go out with my pistol." Laurel headed for the stairs.

Allie's mouth hung open and she closed it. "Be careful."

Laurel had expected a protest. Her sister had probably hoped their father would do something but knowing he was injured, there wasn't much he could do, though it seemed he was well enough for work, which went to ease the weight on her shoulders.

She donned a navy wool dress, sturdy boots, and a jacket. With her pistol at her side, she ventured into the yard out the kitchen door. It was a gray day. Clouds dimmed all color from the earth. What was usually a vibrant festival of green was now a mishmash of browns. Winter was fast on the heels of autumn, though there were weeks left of the colorful season.

If there had been a dog outside of the window, there was no sign of him now. She couldn't place any prints or other signs someone had been there. It was as though the dog had vanished. Allie's omen was invading space in Laurel's mind.

Nobody was going to die.

The world couldn't be cruel enough to take another person from her this year, but she couldn't deny she believed her sister.

She set her pistol in her reticule and headed to the graveyard. If her father asked, the dog had gone in that direction. He wouldn't approve of her chasing down the canine, but it was better than directly disobeying him.

The well-worn path was strewn with leaves, and they swished under her boots like her skirts. She doubted anything would come from her trip to the graveyard but on that occasion, she needed her mother more than anything and she didn't have anywhere else to go.

As she neared the grave, a tight, overwhelming pressure seized her chest. She gritted her teeth, ignoring the feeling. Nobody would hurt her in the graveyard in the light of day. Her fear must be a holdover from her time there the previous night.

"My dear, what are you doing out here?"

Laurel spun around, nearly colliding with the Reverend. He was in full dress as though he was awaiting a service, which was most likely the case. His black hair with gray wingtips was slicked back to perfection, and his brown eyes studied her with deepening creases.

"Good morning, Reverend." She curtsied, feeling strangely odd and out of place. "I thought I would visit my mother."

His eyes widened, and then he sighed. "Of course." He cleared his throat. "Be careful out here. Mr. Boswell was killed out here last night. We will have to hire a constable."

"How horrible." Her hand covered her mouth as if she was shocked. "You don't think the killer is still out here, do you?"

He shook his head. "All the same, you should head home. It isn't safe for a young lady to travel without a chaperone, especially in a secluded area like this."

"I will head straight home after I see my mother."

"See that you do." He gave her a sad smile. "Give my regards to your family. It's a shame you take after your mother. She was a free spirit, but it cost her in the end."

Laurel sucked in a breath. She had heard much the same from the Reverend and the rest of Tenwich, but usually, they weren't so open with their criticism. Her mother was a free spirit, but it didn't make her bad, and it had nothing to do with the circumstances around her death.

Her mother had lost herself years ago, and the only thing that had brought her peace was death. As much as it pained Laurel, she admitted that wherever her mother was now, it was a better place. Nobody was there to judge her, and her mind could no longer torment her.

The Reverend walked away without a reply from Laurel, though she believed his concern to be genuine. The man had his faults, but he was always there for the parish. It wasn't his fault that her mother committed an unforgivable sin.

When she reached the grave, she cursed herself for neglecting to bring flowers. She glanced around, hoping to see some type of floral growth. Instead, her gaze caught something that sucked the oxygen from her lungs.

A canine footprint.

Her first thought was that Allie couldn't see that far from the house, but the footprint was in dried mud, so it wasn't new. It couldn't be more than a few days old, but that didn't explain anything. It must be a loose dog, but a dog that size could account for what Allie saw.

She shivered. It was only a print, and yet, she had seen ghosts and witches. How much of a stretch was a demon dog?

The cold seeped into her bones and she hugged herself. Her mother would understand why she couldn't stay. She checked that she still had her pistol and just as she was putting it away, the leaves crunched behind her.

She spun, aiming the pistol at the sound.

"What do you think you're doing? It's daylight." Conner raised his hands before him.

"I…" Could she tell him about the dog? If anyone would understand, it would be him. "What are you doing here?"

"I suspect the same as you. I came to visit my mother."

"You spend an inordinate amount of them in the graveyard?"

He laughed. "I do? Perhaps we have that in common. Why were you carrying a pistol? The grave robbers are only coming at night."

She bit her lip. "There was a dog."

He froze. "What kind of dog?"

"A big one. I saw it the other night too."

"Why didn't you tell me?"

She shrugged. "I didn't think anything of it. I'm

still not sure it means anything. Someone's dog must have gotten loose."

He shook his head. "Nobody owns that dog."

"Then, you've seen it?"

He frowned. "Not recently, which is puzzling if you are seeing it."

"My sister, too."

"I always thought there was something about Allie. She hides it well, though."

Laurel nodded. "She knows things, like my mother."

"It's curious your gift isn't stronger."

"My gift? You think seeing ghosts is a gift?"

"My mother thought so." He studied her. "Did you drink or eat anything before seeing the dog?"

"No, but I didn't see the dog this morning."

His eyes flickered from side to side and back to her.

"No Conner. I know what you're thinking. I don't want any more of that stuff."

"Nothing bad will happen. Besides, if I don't see the dog then you probably won't."

She huffed. "That defeats the purpose."

He shook his head. "Not if the dog has a target in mind. I might not be able to see it for a reason."

The hair on her arms rose. "No."

"You don't want to know if something bad is going to happen?"

"It's just a silly dog and a silly superstition. Nobody is going to die." She rubbed her hands over her arms.

"It doesn't always mean death but rapid change."

"How could you possibly know?" Her mouth dried.

She knew the answer to her question but couldn't bring herself to trust his authority. It was only a dog.

"I know you don't want to believe me, but it must have something to do with your family. You and Allie both saw it. Could you tell what it was doing?"

"Hunting." She didn't have to think twice about it. The dog had been sniffing around like it was looking for something.

"Did it see you?"

She swallowed. "Yes."

"Curious." He sighed. "There is only one way to know for sure."

"I said no, Conner."

"Would you rather I ask Allie?"

"Don't you dare. If you tell Allie, she'll know I talked to you."

He gave her a quizzical look. "But she probably already knows that."

"Yes, but she will feel obligated to say something to my father if you talk to her directly. She keeps her knowledge to herself as did my mother."

"I suppose you have a point. Come with me then."

"Will you leave Allie alone?"

He nodded and beckoned her with the sweep of his hand. "I'll only give you a little."

"You won't leave me?"

"I'll be right there when it happens. If the dog meant to harm you, it probably would have done so by now. I could be wrong, but I don't think you have anything to fear."

"That is not reassuring."

He chuckled. "I've been like this my whole life, nothing is reassuring, but if you face it, then it no longer has power over you."

"I don't know."

He grasped her shoulders in his hands. "You can do this, Laurel."

The warmth of his hands passed through her jacket and traveled the distance to her heart. This was nonsense. She couldn't let him get to her. Yes, he was dashing, dark, and handsome, but he was off-limits, and this was inappropriate.

Still, she laced her arm through his and allowed him to guide her toward Tenwich House. When they reached the edge of the graveyard, they stopped.

"I'll go first. Meet me at the side entrance. Don't worry about the servants, they are discreet. It's what they are hired to do."

She nodded.

"If anyone asks, say you've taken on mending for the house for extra money."

A sour taste climbed her throat. It was believable, and her family was short on funds. So believable, in fact, that she almost asked if she could do their mending, but she checked herself. If he already believed she was low, then that would make her even lower.

He walked off, leaving her to stare after him.

She studied her gloves, noticing the seams were coming undone, and she made a mental note to go over them. She waited another five minutes and set out on her own. As was common at that time of day, the streets were lined with people. It wasn't a market day, but shops were open, and ladies wandered about making calls.

She said hello to everyone she passed and received

smiles and nods in return. She could almost see the workings in their thoughts as they wondered at her feeblemindedness. Some of them, no doubt, wondered why she wasn't in an asylum. The graveyard girl who shunned society.

Chapter 16

Tenwich House didn't appear as imposing as it had in the dark. The side entrance was crammed with servants coming and going. They didn't think anything of her presence and shooed her to the side as they went.

The entryway wasn't as grand as the main entrance, but it was a step up from her home. The hallway was covered in wood-paneling and maroon paint. The grandeur of the house sent her stomach in knots until she spotted Conner waiting for her off of a kitchen wider than her home.

Wordlessly, she followed him out through the kitchen and out into a narrow hallway that led to a small library or study. The space was comprised of bookshelves lining the walls and a writing desk.

She sighed in relief when she realized they weren't headed to his bedchamber. Of course, they were avoiding his father since it was daytime. Lord Tenwich wouldn't approve of her friendship with Conner. Laurel stilled next to a pile of books. She was in so much trouble.

Conner opened a cabinet door set into the desk and pulled out a bottle of green liquid and two glasses. He poured a thimble-sized portion into each glass.

"One thing I hate," he said, "is drinking alone."

He raised his glass and she tapped hers gently against it.

She swallowed the drink without tasting it and refused to flinch.

He poured himself more and tipped the bottle toward her. The playful gleam in his eyes sent her heart skipping, and she poured herself a full glass of absinthe.

Conner laughed into his drink while she downed her own. "Careful, Laurel. We still need to get you home."

"I'll be the judge of what I can and cannot handle."

He shrugged. "At least wait until it kicks in before you make yourself drunk."

She snorted.

Brilliant move, Laurel. Get drunk to impress a man. Very ladylike.

"I'll have you know I am perfectly able to hold my alcohol." *Liar.*

Conner indicated the chair under the desk, and she dropped down onto it.

"Tired?" he asked.

She nodded and sighed, resting her elbow on the desk. She sensed him watching her and she met his gaze. His gray eyes creased as he smiled at her.

"What is it?"

He shook his head. "Nothing."

"Why are you looking at me that way?"

He chuckled. "What way?"

Like you want to devour me.

"That way." Her heart stumbled as his smile grew.

"You're beautiful."

Her breath caught. "That's the absinthe talking." She cast her gaze away.

"It's a compliment. Absinthe or not. You're stunning."

"You must be daft. I'm not any of that. Don't you know I'm the odd girl who lives beside the graveyard?"

He lifted her chin with a finger, forcing their eyes to lock once more. "There is nothing odd about you. You're perfect."

"You're as mad as they say, aren't you?"

He raised a brow. "Madder, I'm sure, but that doesn't mean what I say isn't true."

She shook her head.

"Do you remember that summer?"

Her heart lodged in her throat. "Of course."

"I've been wanting to do this for a long time."

Conner leaned in, claiming her lips with his. A bolt of electricity shot through her, straight to her toes, and she stood. He moved with a finesse she lacked, but guided by instinct, she allowed his lips to conquer hers.

His tongue danced over hers and she mimicked his actions. Warmth pooled between her legs, and she moaned. He combed his fingers through her hair and tugged it loose from its chignon. His hands wandered lower, and he pressed his hips against hers. The evidence of his arousal prodded her belly.

She gasped and stepped back.

"We shouldn't do this."

He panted and ran a hand over her hair. "You're right." His smile didn't reach his eyes.

"It's a bad idea."

He shook his head. "The worst."

"Who knows where it might lead?"

"To the devil, I'm sure."

"To the devil." She stood on tiptoes and found his lips. Passion overcame her and she clasped her hands behind his neck. He let out a soft growl and lifted her onto the desk.

He stroked her nipples through the fabric of her wool dress, and she arched into him, her mind a blind haze of desire.

Conner's movements became frantic, and he lifted her skirts.

She cried out and pushed the fabric down over her legs. "What are you doing?"

His eyes were glazed over. "Do you trust me?"

She studied his features and her heart galloped in her chest. "Yes."

"You shouldn't."

She squealed as he flung her skirts up over his head. Without hesitation, he grasped her hips and lifted her to meet his mouth. She stared wide-eyed at his head tenting her skirts. She had heard about this in one of Maya's novels but couldn't grasp why it was enjoyable.

He started to lick, and her limbs shook. The slow, playful licks of a man savoring the taste of delicate fruit.

"Oh God, Conner." She bucked into him.

His licks increased in speed and her body tightened. She rode him without any room for embarrassment. Her eyes tilted back into her head, and she heard nothing but her heartbeat. His tongue teased and tormented her until her body was at its peak.

Then, he found her center and sucked. She screamed and melted into a pile of quaking limbs. The explosive force of her climax sent aftershocks through her, and he steadied her against the desk.

He kissed her inner thighs and rose from under her skirts.

"That was beautiful, thank you." He kissed her

panting lips.

"What have you done to me?" She smiled through her words.

"I had to taste you."

She blinked and straightened her skirts. She was at a loss for words. This man who had given her pleasure was thanking her. Her legs wobbled as she stood, and Conner kept a hand at her back to prevent her from falling.

Her head swam. The absinthe had kicked in. Of course, why else would she allow him to do such a thing? She would blame that vile green liquid on her lapse in judgment. It was a mistake, but how can something that felt so good be bad?

Laurel combed her fingers through her hair and fastened it in place.

"Are you ready?"

She stared at him a moment, unsure what he was referring to.

"The dog." The side of his lips turned up.

"Yes." The word came out in a dry croak. "I'm always ready."

Conner patted her shoulder and gestured to the exit, but she stared at it with dumb, blinking eyes.

"Before someone comes."

Of course, she had screamed. She shook as she followed him out the door. Nobody seemed to notice them as they passed, but all the same, Laurel's cheeks remained scarlet as she imagined each of them read her expression, which only fueled the heat.

Conner chuckled as they stepped out of Tenwich House and onto a gravel drive.

"See anything?"

She had almost forgotten why they had taken the absinthe. "N…no?"

"It's all right. We will go to the graveyard. It may be a shot in the dark since the dog is probably gone by now."

She swallowed and nodded. "He seemed to prowl around."

You idiot. Of course, he prowled.

Laurel gave him a sheepish smile.

He watched her, his lips still tucked up on one side.

How could he be so unaffected? The man shattered her world and all he could think about was that monstrous dog. What did she want from him? A proposal?

Her face fell. "I'll meet you there." She bolted before he could say another word. She had done enough for one day to ruin herself.

Her boots crunched over the gravel as she hurried forward. All eyes seemed to be on her as she made her way through the marketplace. They couldn't possibly know. Could they? She kept her chin lowered and eyes to the ground, and almost collided with the firm, overly dressed Mr. Masters.

He steadied her with a hand. "Miss Atwell, where are you going to in such a hurry?"

"I'm sorry, sir. I am needed home." She attempted to step past him, but he stopped her with a hand on her elbow.

"Let me escort you. I was about to visit you."

Damn.

She had forgotten he meant to visit, though she had never believed he meant it. She peered up into his clear, blue eyes, and all her words of protest melted.

"Were you? I'm sorry, I had an urgent errand."

He chuckled, revealing a dimple in his left cheek. Could this man be any more perfect? "No need to apologize. I'm here now."

Mr. Masters led her away, her arm settled on his. He managed to weave around deep puddles and offending mud, and by the time they reached her home, her hem was free of dirt and her boots were dry. The man was a marvel.

"Won't you come in?"

Mr. Masters gave her a bright smile. "Delighted."

She settled him in the parlor and put on water for tea. Allie readied a tray of biscuits when she saw her sister's plight and Allie's fiancé, Mr. Cross, joined them.

Laurel worried her lip as she stared out the window, wishing Conner away.

"I hear you're in the family business, Miss Atwood?"

A scratch along the floorboards caught Laurel's attention and she whipped her head up.

Allie raised a brow at Laurel. "Indeed. Mr. Cross and I intend to continue on the family business."

The scratch turned into a whine and Laurel went pale. Nobody else seemed to hear the canine as his claws clicked toward them.

"Oh, that's right. Congratulations." Mr. Masters glowed. She could get trapped in his gaze if it wasn't for the transparent image of her dead dog staring up at her.

This was not the dog she had intended to see, but she couldn't resist the temptation to scratch the beast behind his ear.

All eyes fell on her, and she hid her action with a stretch.

Allie tossed her a warning look. "Thank you, Mr. Masters."

Rollo pawed at her skirts and the animal's claws seemed to rake over her skin. She let out a groan and attempted to brush the dog away, but her fingers slid right through him.

"Is something the matter, Miss Laurel?"

"No, no, nothing." She plastered a smile on her face.

"You seem uncomfortable."

Allie squeezed Laurel's hand. "Perhaps you should lie down. Is it your nerves?"

Laurel let out a dry laugh. "I'm sure it's nothing." She gave Allie a pointed look. Her nerves were as strong as ever, but she couldn't fault her sister for allowing her a way out. If she retired to her room, she would be expected to stay there and the last thing she needed was to miss the effects of the absinthe. She didn't want to go through this again.

"Hmm." Mr. Masters regarded her. "In any case, I came to invite you to a dance at my aunt's, Miss Atwell, Miss Laurel Atwell, and Mr. Cross."

Rollo pawed at her, this time as though he were running up her leg. She swallowed back a yelp and bit her tongue.

"Isn't that lovely?" Allie said.

"Delightful," Laurel squeaked. Rollo renewed his attacks on her leg.

Mr. Masters rose from his place across from the ladies. "It's settled then. I will see you all this Saturday." He beamed at Laurel.

"Stop that." She waved a hand over the ghost.

The room fell silent.

Laurel laughed nervously. "I'm sorry."

"Are you sure you're all right?" Mr. Masters frowned. His handsome face didn't transform into a hideous creature, but instead, he was even more handsome.

She sighed. "My nerves." She silently thanked Allie for the idea.

He nodded in understanding. "Do invite your father as well. I hear he has been unwell, but I'd love to speak with him if he is available."

A chill rushed over Laurel's skin. She had recently met this man and he wanted to speak to her father. Hopefully, it was about business or hunting, and not to ask for her hand.

Her legs turned to putty, and she sat herself down after Mr. Masters made his excuses. The man was an Adonis. Perfection itself. Yet, she didn't want to marry him, especially on such short acquaintance.

Allie sat beside her. "He's sniffing you out, Laurel." She beamed at her sister. "I knew you would make the superior match."

She would finally be able to help her family. Wasn't this what she wanted?

Chapter 17

With a brief hug and a warm smile, Allie led Mr. Cross back to the workshop. Laurel couldn't make sense of Mr. Masters' visit or Conner's attentions even if she was a beauty, which she didn't believe, she wasn't marriage material. Someone must have duped Mr. Masters into believing she had a handsome dowry, but from where she couldn't fathom.

She allowed her muscles to loosen and went for the front door, avoiding the area of the workshop. She had shrouds to sew before the end of the day and the absinthe would wear off. Hopefully, she would, or rather wouldn't, see the dog.

Rollo barked at her. It was a hollow sound, like someone speaking from another room. She attempted to scratch him behind the ear, but her hand went through the apparition. It was curious that she could touch him sometimes, and other times, her hands passed right through.

"Rollo, come." She ushered the dog ahead of her out the door.

She glanced toward the workshop, but the area was still and luckily the window faced away from the graveyard or she would have to explain her actions to her father. She had already taken the chance he wouldn't notice her missing this morning.

She set out down the path, Rollo at her heels. Her

chest was near bursting with dread and excitement at seeing Conner again. What they did shouldn't have happened. Why couldn't she gain interest in someone like Mr. Masters? The man was untitled, which meant he was more available to her, but Conner would inherit his father's title, which left her without any hope of securing him.

Perhaps it was his unavailability that made him so attractive. She had often wondered if she would be happy as a wife and mother, but what choice did she have? Her family needed her, and Mr. Masters wasn't only her best option, he was her only option, and that made him a less enticing choice.

Besides Rollo, no ghosts appeared as she wandered into the graveyard. Conner was right. They didn't seem to roam there. She scanned the area, but Conner wasn't in view.

Her middle clenched. Had he tired of her after their intimate moment? She shook her head. The trees seemed to creep up on them as they passed gravestones, each one leading them deeper into the forest. She hadn't realized where she was taking them until they neared the small clearing where the witches had practiced.

She didn't know what she expected. Not a soul, dead or otherwise, was present. If it wasn't for Rollo at her side, she would have assumed the absinthe had worn off. What had happened to her mother's ghost? Had it been a dream?

A blackened-out pit stood in the center of the clearing, and she pushed the ashes around with her boot. A hint of some herb wafted up from the ashes and she inhaled the heady scent. It was unidentifiable to her, but she decided it must have some similar properties as absinthe. She was no cook or healer, so it was unlikely she would identify the plant if it was staring her in the face.

She dug deeper into the pit with the toe of her boot and kicked up the edge of a familiar shoe. Her mother's slipper, but how had it gotten here? Was it the same one the Reverend had brought her father that he threw in the fire? If that were the case, she imagined her father must know about the witches.

Laurel's throat tightened. Her father wouldn't have anything to do with witches. He wasn't a religious man, but he thought of witchcraft as nonsense. Why would he surrender the slipper to them? Or perhaps they had taken it?

Which led her to wonder, had the witches taken her mother? It was the logical conclusion, and she had considered it before, but the sensations she had felt when in their presence had left her in denial.

She buried the remains of the shoe in the bits of charred wood and a tear pushed its way past her lashes. Her body slumped as she remembered the past few days full of tears and wonder. Regardless of what her father wanted, Conner had taken her out of her slump. He had given her purpose and joy when the world seemed hollow.

She dashed away her tears and took a deep breath.

"It's almost as though nothing had happened." Conner came up beside her.

"You don't see them either?"

He quirked a brow. "I see that old dog of yours. What was his name? Rollo?"

She sighed. "I don't know what's gone wrong."

He studied her. "They must have moved on, but

that would mean someone must have intervened."

"The witches?"

He flinched. "Possibly, but the Reverend could have too."

"Or anyone else who had any knowledge, for that matter. Are you sure you didn't do something?"

He blinked and then squinted his eyes. "I would have said something."

"As far as I know, you just wanted to get me drunk."

"You're being ridiculous. The absinthe hadn't had a chance yet. I don't need you drunk to seduce you." He leaned over her, his lips closing on hers.

She made an abrupt step back and slapped his cheek. "Don't you dare."

"Ouch." His hand went to his cheek. "You seemed to enjoy it before."

"It was a momentary lapse in judgment." She swallowed back her embarrassment, but the warmth between her legs screamed at her to submit. "I don't need you to tell me what I enjoy. You're the worst kind of scoundrel preying on vulnerable women."

She had been weak from stress and likely drunk. What had he been thinking? Of course, he had drunk the absinthe too.

He let out a faint laugh. "If that's what you want." He turned away from her.

Words caught in her throat. She raised a hand, wanting to stop him, to beg him for forgiveness, but she didn't. He earned that slap and if she could go back in time and erase that moment in the study, if she could replay it again, she would have slapped him then too.

He had no business seducing her. She needed a

husband, not a lover. He couldn't be that for her.

"I don't need you," she shouted after him.

He waved a hand over his shoulder.

She swallowed back the new tears that had gathered. Had she gone too far? It was an innocent kiss between friends, right? What they had done hadn't been innocent, but what he was about to do, well, it couldn't happen.

Laurel slumped down on a log next to the charred remains of her mother's slipper. She stared at Rollo, who scratched his transparent ear.

"You understand, don't you?"

Rollo wagged his tail.

"I don't know what has come over me, but whatever that was needed to end. I can't have him around if I'm going to pursue someone like Mr. Masters."

The dog barked.

"You agree?" She sighed. "I wanted to marry for love." She shrugged. "My family needs me."

Rollo nudged against her, and she thought she felt the scraggly mane of the creature. They stayed like that for a while when Laurel resigned herself to returning. At last, she had burned that bridge with Conner, and she could return to her father without the weight of guilt.

Yet, different guilt had settled like a heavy pit in her stomach. More than likely, Conner had been innocent of her accusations. He had seduced her. That was enough to earn him a slap, but she had wanted his attention. No, she encouraged his attention.

She found her feet and motioned for Rollo to follow, but the dog had disappeared. The loss of her friend drained her energy, but she continued on the path back to the graveyard. Her mother had been especially fond of Rollo, often favoring the dog over her children. He was part of the family as much as Laurel was.

Laurel let the leaves crush under her boots and passed each grave without any acknowledgment. Her choice had crushed her breast to the point she wasn't sure her heart still beat, but she would live without Conner as she had for years.

She gathered her shawl about her and kicked up the leaves in her way. Mr. Masters would make a fine husband, and she would do everything she could to learn to be a dutiful wife, even if it meant giving up her graveyard wanderings and her shroud work.

The screen door thumped behind her as she entered the kitchen. The remains of a fire still burned in the hearth. She stoked the dying flames to life and settled at the table. Without any prodigy, she decided to ready everyone's lunch.

She cut sections of meat and cheese leftover from the night before and sliced a fresh loaf of bread Allie had baked that morning. Then, she poured some beer for each place at the table. By the time Allie, her father, and Mr. Cross arrived, she had created a fine assortment of foods for them to enjoy. Fruits and jellies with nuts and biscuits accompanied the meal.

Allie stood frozen in the doorway. "You did all this?"

A small smile touched her lips and she nodded.

"It's wasteful," her father said.

Her smile fell and she rubbed a hand over her arm.

"It's delightful, Laurel. Thank you."

Mr. Cross nodded to Laurel and took his place next to Allie.

Her father dug into the meal but eyed her while he chewed. "What is this about?"

She spread jelly over a slice of bread. "I have to learn to run a household. It is the least I can do while everyone is in the workshop."

"You sew shrouds," Allie pointed out.

"True, but that won't keep everyone fed. Sure, it gives us a little income, but it won't sustain a busy household."

Her father cleared his throat. "You also must be aware of the extent of the larder and the budget. This will get us through the afternoon but what of the evening? Should we eat the same fare or eat tomorrow's food?"

Her throat was dry as she struggled to swallow the bread.

"Enough, father. She's trying." Allie gave her a weak smile.

"I just thought that—"

He snorted. "You thought wrong."

Laurel finished the rest of her meal in silence and cleaned up after the feast with numb fingers. She couldn't do something as simple as prepare a meal. How was she going to be a wife? A mother? Allie was more suited to the role and yet, Allie had the workshop.

She was so used to caring for her ailing mother and the deceased that she hadn't had a chance to learn to care for the living. She steadied herself against the cabinets and finished the chores. At least, the dead didn't complain if her hems were straight.

She let out a laugh.

Laurel entered the parlor where she had left her

sewing. The basket was higher than it had been yesterday. More mending and death.

She closed her eyes and took a deep breath. It was how she dealt with that foreboding sensation she got with sewing shrouds, but as much as it hurt, she would sew the shrouds even if she wasn't paid. Everyone deserved the quality of her stitches in death. Everyone deserved an elegant send-off.

Now, she was one step closer to helping her family. She hadn't found her mother's body, or Mr. Boswell's killer, or even the demon dog, but she had gained a suitor, who would make so much more of life bearable. She could move on with her life and do away with childish things. Her mother would understand.

Yet, she couldn't help but wonder whether she meant Mr. Masters or Conner Woodward.

Chapter 18

An hour later, Maya had joined her in the parlor. They sat close enough to whisper for fear of being overheard by her father or Allie in the workshop. Maya had heard about Mr. Masters' visit and wanted all the details. Instead, Laurel had unburdened herself of information about Conner and the ghosts.

"It isn't like that." Laurel pushed her needle through the fabric.

Maya's eyes widened. "Then what is it like?"

She knew she shouldn't have said anything. With everything left unsaid, Maya could smell scandal from a parish away. What she had shared with Conner was over. Why had she insisted on telling Maya anything, even if it was a glossed over version of the truth? "We are just friends. We were friends anyway."

Maya's mouth dropped open. "You slept with him, didn't you?"

Laurel jabbed her finger. "Ouch." She sucked on the wound. "What makes you think that?"

"Your face is the color of a poppy."

Laurel diverted her gaze, finding the parlor drapes interesting all of a sudden. "I didn't sleep with him."

"Then what? And don't lie to me." Maya set down her needlework, which she had long since ignored.

"Should we be having this conversation? What if Allie walks in? Or worse, my father?"

"Then you better hurry." A mischievous twinkle lit behind Maya's eyes.

"I'm not saying anything. The point is: I can see ghosts."

Maya waved a hand. "So?"

"There are witches, Maya."

She snorted. "I already knew that."

Laurel blinked at her. "How? What do you know about them?"

Maya scrunched up her nose. "They practice in the forest beyond the graveyard, like you said. I've seen them on full moons sometimes."

"You saw them? What were you doing in the forest at night?"

Maya gave her a level stare. "There isn't much privacy anywhere else. Besides, I've been invited on a number of occasions, but it isn't for me."

Laurel dropped her mending. "When were you planning to tell me this?"

"I didn't think it was important, and I thought you knew. You're the one who spends so much time in the graveyard. You had to have seen them on more than one occasion. It's no matter."

"Don't you see? They could be the ones taking the bodies?"

"That's doubtful. What would they want with bodies?"

"Don't witches sacrifice people to the devil?"

Maya sighed. "Of course not. These witches are older than that. The coven in Tenwich has been around since before Christianity set foot in England. You're talking about different witches. These ones are peaceful."

"Different witches? Maya, how do you know these things?"

Maya frowned. "I don't recall. Though I think it must have been Sally Reed. She knows all about these things. You'll have to ask her."

Sally Reed, of all people. The woman hated Laurel as much as she hated her ever since Laurel had splashed her at Amber Pond. God forbid she mess up the princess's perfect hair. Every time she came across Sally now, the woman would spout lies just loud enough for Laurel to hear. It didn't seem to matter how many times Laurel had apologized.

"Isn't there anyone else?"

Maya twisted up her lips. "Not that I recall." She gave Laurel a toothy grin. Her friend knew perfectly well the two women didn't get along. "Tell me more about Conner."

Laurel lowered her brows. "There isn't anything to tell. We parted ways."

"Because he tried to kiss you?" Maya shook her head. "I don't know what goes on in that brain of yours. At least, you have Mr. Masters' attention. I told you that you could do it." Maya squeezed Laurel's hand. "What is it? You don't look happy."

She shrugged. "It isn't that. I should be in mourning, not looking for a husband, but father insists." Every day she missed her mother like she would miss breathing. Even though her mother hadn't been herself in years, the presence of her had been a comfort she had always been able to turn to. Now, the place where her mother had been was empty.

"Laurel, you have been mourning. You've been grieving your mother for years. It just took time before death sank in. Besides, Mrs. Atwell would approve of your suitors."

"Suitors? Conner is not a suitor."

"Oh pish. If the man wanted to kiss you, after all that ghost nonsense, then he'll come back after a little slap. I'm surprised he kept around as long as he did. Most men would run screaming once they found out you saw your mother."

Laurel glared at her. "You didn't go running."

"Yet." Maya smiled. "Remember, I'm your best friend and I'm here to put up with whatever mad things you say, such as Conner not being a suitor."

"He's not. I mean, I enjoyed my time with him, but he's too far above me to be an option, and sleeping with him would be a mistake." Never mind she had nearly done just that.

"You keep telling me that, but I know you, and I know how society works. You won't be satisfied until you get a taste of him."

Laurel choked on a laugh, her face burning.

"There." Maya pointed at her. "You slept with him. I knew it."

"Slept with who?" Allie entered the room, her mouth twitching into a smile.

"Conner," Maya whispered.

Allie's brows raised. "Laurel, how could you do something so stupid?"

"I didn't." Laurel gritted her teeth. "I swear. It isn't what you think."

Allie studied her. "I'll have to talk with him. He must do the honorable thing by you."

"Neither of you believe me," Laurel huffed. "It wasn't like that at all."

Allie came up beside her and set a hand on her shoulder. "What happened?"

Laurel's face was flushed, and her palms sweat. "I don't want to talk about it."

Allie's brows continued their ascent up her forehead. "Laurel, what you did was inexcusable, but at least you won't become pregnant."

"Oh my God, Allie. Don't say another word."

"What?" Maya climbed off her chair.

Allie whispered something in Maya's ear.

Maya's eyes widened. "I knew it." She studied Laurel's expression. "It's nothing to be ashamed of, but the man owes you."

"He owes me?" Laurel scrunched up her nose.

"He can't do something like that and walk away from it. You're an innocent, Laurel. A lady, and he can't take that away from you without consequences."

"I'm not a lady."

Allie sighed. "It doesn't matter your title. We're all ladies, and he must answer for this."

"Please don't say anything to father."

Allie eyed her. "He wouldn't understand if I did. He hates the Woodwards more than anyone, and his answer to this would be burning Conner at the stake. What were you thinking?"

Maya chuckled. "She wasn't thinking. At least, not with her head."

"Maya, you aren't helping."

Her friend raised her hands as though in surrender and gathered her things. "Talk to Sally, Laurel." She tugged on her gloves. "She'll tell you everything." Maya let herself out the door, a slight smirk on her face.

Allie rounded on Laurel. "What a mess you've

made."

"Do you have to talk to him?"

"If, or rather, when this gets out, you'll be ruined."

"Nobody saw us." Laurel's words came out weaker than she intended. She crossed the room to stare out the window.

"That doesn't mean anything. Servants talk. Someone was bound to hear something and put two and two together. Laurel, brace yourself for what's to come. If you don't marry soon, you won't marry at all, and you'll bring us all down with you."

"Mr. Cross?"

Allie shook her head. "I don't know what he'll do."

"But we know exactly what father will do. He'd rather see me ruined than join with the Woodward family. Allie, you have to keep this a secret. Nobody has to know, and who's to say anyone will believe the servants."

Seconds ticked by as Allie hesitated.

"Please. I promise I'll give Mr. Masters a chance, and by the time our courtship is established, nobody will even think of Conner Woodward."

Allie bit her lip. "I suppose you're right. I don't believe the Woodwards would do the honorable thing."

"You don't like them either?" She supposed she shouldn't like Conner. He had shown himself to be as careless as his father. Yet, he saw her. He didn't only relate to her experiences, but he saw who she was. Mr. Masters only seemed to skim the surface of their relationship. True, it was all new to them, and Conner had a head start, but she couldn't imagine knowing anyone the same way she knew Conner.

What was she doing? She was supposed to be

getting herself out of this mess with Conner, not digging herself a deeper hole.

"It isn't whether I like them or not. It's whether you do."

"I don't know. I don't remember much about the family. All I know is Conner and he's always been decent to me." If by some stroke of luck, the Woodwards would want her, she would still lose her father, and that was not negotiable.

Allie sighed. "I'll keep it quiet, but at the first sniff of gossip, we're taking you straight to Tenwich House with or without father's consent."

Laurel rushed forward and wrapped her arms around her sister. She squeezed her until it was as if every bit of gratitude powered her grasp.

"Okay, let me breathe." Allie stepped back and studied her. "Do remember we have a dance to prepare for? I hope you have something suitable to wear."

Laurel squeezed her eyes shut. The dance. She had completely forgotten the dance at Lady Quinn's house. According to Maya, everyone in Tenwich had been invited to the event, or at least, everyone who was anyone, according to Maya. The dance was to be the highlight of life in Tenwich until midwinter, and she hadn't prepared.

Allie rolled her eyes. "You should wear the blue."

"Aren't we supposed to be in mourning?" The blue gown was closer to green, but Allie liked to pretend she wasn't matching every dress with Laurel's pale green eyes. It was something their mother had started when Laurel was in the schoolroom.

"Finding a suitor for you is far more important. We can't afford to be in mourning. You're only trying to get out of this dance. You should be excited. Mr. Masters is a lovely man."

"He's perfect." Laurel didn't mean it as a compliment. The man was too perfect. Even his dimples depressed in just the right way to make any girl's legs melt beneath her. "It's just I don't know what I'm doing anymore."

Allie smiled. "I see Conner Woodward has scrambled your brain." She looked deep into Laurel's eyes. "Husband. You."

Laurel nodded. "You're right. It isn't that difficult, but why does it feel like the earth is trying to swallow me?"

"Those are nerves, dear." Allie chuckled. "I had them."

"You did?"

"You think I was always sure about Mr. Cross?" Allie shook her head. "Far from it. Marriage is one of the most important decisions of your life. It shouldn't be made lightly. I didn't just choose Mr. Cross because we're suited. He will help continue the family business and the family I've always wanted."

"I'm happy for you. I am, but I don't know if marriage is right for me."

Allie regarded her with a patient smile. "It is. You'll know when it is right when the time comes. Hopefully, it comes sooner rather than later. We need this, Laurel."

"No pressure."

"No pressure."

Laurel settled down next to her mending basket and took up her work while Allie left for the workshop. Her sister had always been kind and supportive of

Laurel, and the gentle nudge she had given her was more of a firm shove from Allie.

She stared at the basket, wishing it would disappear so she could wander the graveyard, but she had taken too many chances today. Anymore and she would be courting disaster with her father. From now on, she would be a dutiful daughter. Allie was right, she needed to get married whether or not it was Mr. Masters.

She would allow Conner to find the grave robber and murderer. Better yet, she would suggest to the Reverend that they hire a Bow Street runner from town. Something had to be done about the corpses, but she would forget about ghosts and witches. What nonsense. She had lived comfortably not knowing about them before.

This dance would go a long way to help her find a match. In the least, it would bring her closer to Mr. Masters, but it would also acquaint her with the man's friends who would be invited from outside of Tenwich, and she had exhausted the men of Tenwich.

All she had to do was forget about Conner Woodward and this time, it would have to stick. They had gone too far. The man was a dangerous influence on her. He not only accepted her disobeying her father, he encouraged it. She would hold fast this time. Already she had taken the first step to thwart his advances.

Luckily, it was unlikely that the man was invited to the dance, but what Laurel forget to realize was that overlooking the Woodwards was not something Lady Quinn was prepared to do with the most important family in Tenwich.

Chapter 19

The day of the dance loomed heavy. Laurel kept picking and smoothing her dress until her hands were numb from the effort. Her gown was from last season, but it would suit in Tenwich. She had no need for glamorous clothes there.

Allie helped arrange her hair in braids that she placed into a stunning updo. The blue gown, as she called it, was a high-waist number with gauzy bubbled sleeves and matching blue-green slippers. Allie lent her a pair of paste earrings that looked remarkably like sapphires alone with a similar necklace that seemed to float on her collarbone.

She finished her outfit with gloves fashioned to the elbows and smiled at the effect in the mirror. Behind her, Allie offered a reassuring pat on her back before slipping away to prepare her own ensemble.

"Don't let it get to your head." Allie laughed. "You look beautiful."

Laurel beamed. "Thanks to you."

"I don't tell you often enough, but you would look good in sackcloth. You tend to forget that."

Laurel waved a hand. "You're required to say that as my sister."

"As your sister, I'm required to tell you the truth."

"Lies." She shooed Allie from the room. This was the part she would turn to Rollo and ask for his advice, but the dog was gone once again.

She sighed and wished she had more absinthe, but without Conner, she had no access to the alcohol. Her father didn't drink anything stronger than beer, but she doubted her family could afford it, anyway. Perhaps Maya knew where she could find some.

She had never dreamed she would step foot in Lady Quinn's mansion, and once she did, she wondered how so much space could go unused for so long. The checkered marble floors in the entryway gave way to polished pearl-hued marble in the ballroom. Hundreds of candles lit the room, inviting guests to mingle.

A screen was set up detailing the labors of Hercules in front of the musicians. Rubber plants flanked the screen and the refreshment table hosted an assortment of biscuits and tiny sandwiches as well as a weak lemonade.

Her usual neighbors surrounded her as well as some young bucks she didn't recognize as well as a few dandies. Her gaze continued to scan the crowd when she locked gazes with Conner Woodward.

Her breath hitched, and he stepped in her direction just as Maya pulled her to the side.

"What is he doing here?" she hissed.

Maya blinked. "He's from the most important family in the parish, what did you expect?"

"I expected him to stay away." He had for years. Why must tonight be any different?

"Just ignore him. Mr. Masters has been asking for you."

Ignore Conner Woodward? Impossible. The man was larger than other men, not because he was taller, he wasn't. Or because he was wider, he wasn't. Conner took up space the same way that cats licked up cream. He owned the room, and nobody could take it from him.

Maya led her straight into the arms of Mr. Masters, who offered for the first dance of the evening. They lined up with the other couples and curtsied. Down the row, Conner exchanged bows with his own partner.

The dance progressed and the steps flew by as Laurel attempted to keep her attention on her partner, but Conner's gray eyes seemed to follow her across the floor. She took extra care with each movement but the sensation of being watched crowded her until the end of the dance, and she reined in her speed as she fled the dance floor with Mr. Masters trailing her.

She pulled up in front of her father. Allie had joined the next dance and he was alone. Mr. Masters joined them.

"The nerve of that man showing up." Her father nodded his head toward Conner. "He should know better."

"I apologize, Mr. Atwell. My aunt insisted on inviting the Woodwards."

"And where is your aunt? I haven't seen her yet."

Mr. Masters grinned. "I'm afraid she's battling a headache."

Her father quirked a brow. "Is she? I suppose you can't be persuaded to throw him out?"

Mr. Masters leaned toward her father. "I want nothing more, but you know I can't."

"It would be most improper," Laurel said.

"If only he would show himself for who he is." Her father cast a glare in her direction.

"And how is that, father?"

He smoothed a hand over her own. "My pet, I know you're taken with the boy, but he's not worth your time or heartbreak."

She stilled. Her father had been perceptive, and too much so. She faced Mr. Masters, hoping to explain herself, but the man had his attention elsewhere. All the eyes in the room had turned. A raven-haired beauty had entered the room.

She seemed to glow as she made her way down the stairs. Her fuchsia gown ended in an elegant train behind her. Her stunning alabaster skin was near translucent and for a moment Laurel wondered if she was a vampire. Ghosts and witches existed, why not vampires?

At the bottom of the stairs, Conner assisted her, and the crush of men began.

"Who is that?" Laurel whispered.

"Miss Amelia Woodward." Mr. Masters appeared to catch his breath. "I didn't believe she would attend."

"Conner's sister?" her father asked.

"Cousin, I believe."

Laurel's heart thudded. "First cousin?"

Mr. Masters shook his head. "Distant cousin, but their families are close."

Her heart seemed to deplete as Conner led Miss Woodward onto the dance floor. They were a fitting match. Her stomach flip-flopped as his eyes seemed to capture every inch of Miss Woodward.

At that time, Mr. Masters found a new partner, and her father went to get more weak lemonade. Maya appeared beside her, frowning.

"You can't let her get away with it."

Laurel sighed. "I'm doing no such thing."

"Then why are you standing here? Go take back what is yours."

She gave her friend a level look. "He isn't mine, and he never will be."

"Not with that attitude. Come, I'll distract the she-demon and you whisk your man away to a nearby corner. Then wedding bells."

Laurel coughed on a laugh. "You can't be serious." On the surface, the plan was sound, but she would be ruined before her father would allow such a thing, and she would lose her chance with Mr. Masters. "Maya, there are plenty of attractive men here."

"Boys. They are boys. Some of them only returning from Eton."

"You would say the same about Mr. Woodward."

Maya pointed a finger at her. "That is different. He isn't for me. Yes, he's young but he has the power to back him up."

She crossed her arms. "Only what his father gave him."

Maya stuck out her lower lip. "I thought you liked him."

"It doesn't matter whether I like him or not. I can't have him. My father would have apoplexy if I pursued it any further."

"Fine. Settle for Mr. Masters, but you would make an excellent Lady."

Laurel dropped her hands as the man in question approached. She caught Conner's eyes and all sound fell away. His confidence glowed as did his cousin's, who rested her hand on his arm.

"Miss Woodward, Miss Meadows. Allow me to introduce my cousin, Miss Woodward."

They exchanged curtsies but Laurel never dropped her gaze from his.

"It's a pleasure, Miss Woodward." She smoothed her gloved hands over her skirts to steady her nerves. Why had he introduced his cousin? Was it to rub her nose in it? She plastered on a smile.

"We were just talking about you." Maya grinned.

"Oh?" Even Amelia's voice was enchanting, a decadent honey sound.

Laurel shot her a look.

"Indeed. Your dress is stunning."

Miss Woodward gave them a small smile. "Thank you."

"Of course, my father would kill me if I tried to carry off such a dress. It is, what would you call it, Laurel? Indecent?"

Laurel coughed to disguise a laugh and slammed her elbow into her friend's side. "I wouldn't call it indecent."

"Wasn't that what you were saying?" Maya blinked her lashes.

"I think it's lovely."

Miss Woodward's full lips tugged up. "I'll have to give you the name of my modiste in town." She nodded to Laurel. "Of course, I don't know if you would be able to afford her."

Laurel's mouth fell open, and Maya pushed her aside.

"There is hardly a need for such clothes in Tenwich," Maya said.

"I can see that." Miss Woodward directed her smile at Conner. "Cousin, the next dance starts."

Conner looked between them, shook his head, and

led her away.

"The nerve." Maya gritted her teeth.

Laurel sighed. "Maya, you did it again."

"What? I did nothing. She was the one who came prancing into the ballroom on the most eligible man's arm like she owned the place."

"She's a guest."

"She took your man."

Laurel lowered her voice. "He isn't my man. She is free to do whatever she wishes with him." A solid mass like a horse's hoof lodged into her stomach. He wasn't hers. He never would be. Best to get it over with.

"What is wrong with you, Laurel? When you were spending time with him, you were glowing, and I couldn't get a dozen words out of you without you mentioning him. Now, he might as well be horse dung. Did something happen?"

Reality had happened. There was nothing between them and there never was, but she didn't want to argue with Maya anymore. Her best friend was her greatest ally, but also her biggest critic. When Maya found a painful spot, she doused it with salt and then dressed it with salve. It was an unusual friendship, but it worked.

"You know as much as I do."

"That's sad."

"What's sad?" Mr. Masters joined them, and his hair seemed to shine with the brightness of his smile.

Maya perked up. "It's sad Laurel doesn't have a partner for the next dance."

Mr. Masters bowed. "Allow me to remedy that."

"Mr. Masters, two dances? What will people think?" Laurel glanced toward Conner but failed to meet his gaze.

"Whatever they want." He offered his arm, and she placed her hand on it. "The next dance is a waltz."

Laurel stopped short. "You can't be serious. I don't think I can manage."

"It's easy. If you allow me to lead, everything will be perfect."

The man was an excellent dancer as she had noted earlier, but she hadn't expected a waltz. It was scandalous for Tenwich. What had Lady Quinn been thinking?

"Look He gestured to the dance floor. All the other couples are lining up."

She licked her lips. "All right." She followed his lead onto the floor and his hand took hers. His other hand rested on her waist. Her heart skipped, and she remembered it wasn't Conner who led the dance, though she spotted him with Miss Woodward on the other side of the room, readying to dance.

The musicians played the first notes of the waltz, and Mr. Masters swirled her about. It was effortless, leaving room for conversation, but Laurel couldn't focus on any word he said. Her gaze was locked on Conner.

The man's attention was caught on his cousin. Every time she faced him, she willed him to meet her gaze to show her what they had experienced wasn't false. With every turn, her heart clenched tighter in her chest.

Mr. Masters spoke. "I apologize for his presence."

She shook her head. "It's nothing."

"The way you are watching them, I expect he was responsible for killing your favorite kitten. I didn't mean to offend you."

Her lips made a thin line. "You did what you had to do." She met his gaze.

"It's refreshing, you understand." He sighed. "I've been searching for a woman like you for a long time."

She tripped on her shoes. "Like me?"

His smile would melt mountains. "Just like you."

Her eyes stung and her stomach flopped. "Excuse me. I have a sudden headache." She extracted herself from his grip and fled the ballroom to the not too quiet whispers around her.

The terrace was lit with scattered lanterns and the light of the almost full moon. She ignored the chill that accompanied the open air, but she shivered all the same. Beyond the terrace, a deep green garden hid the yard, and likely, wayward couples. The thought only made her posture sag further.

Nothing could be more perfect than the conversation she had just had. Nothing could sway the now falling tears coating her face as she rushed onto the terrace. Nothing, of course, besides Conner Woodward.

She was a fool for mourning a man she couldn't have when a perfect specimen had come to claim her. But yet, for all of Mr. Masters' polished charm, she was left with a sour taste in the back of her throat. He was perfect, but he didn't light a fire in her heart. She hated herself for not feeling the way she should for a happy marriage.

She let her shoulders sag and waited for some well-meaning person to come escort her back to the dance. She expected Maya, or maybe Mr. Masters himself, but instead, the gorgeous raven-haired beauty, Miss

Woodward, rushed to her side. Conner was nowhere to be seen.

Chapter 20

Miss Woodward took a place beside her overlooking the silent garden. Her raven hair caught on the breeze, giving an illusion that she wasn't vampiric at all but fairy-like. The woman watched her with startling blue eyes.

"I thought you would come out here." Miss Woodward tipped her head to the side. "It's a nice night."

Laurel sucked in a breath. "It is."

"It isn't my place, but are you all right?" Concern creased her eyes.

"I'm quite so. I'm only overwhelmed." So many things had happened in the past few weeks she couldn't get a grasp of her own emotions, and worst of all, she wasn't given the space to do so.

"It is rather warm in there."

Laurel faced her. "It isn't just that." She studied the other woman's face and decided to take a leap. "Do you believe in ghosts?" Her ability had nagged at her since seeing her mother. She needed to know she wasn't crazy.

A grin claimed Miss Woodward's lips. "Of course. It's the family secret, you know. Not so much a secret."

"Then it isn't only Con— Mr. Woodward?"

Miss Woodward's grin grew wider. "Most of us can see ghosts. Not the Woodwards, but everyone. Our

173

family happens to acknowledge it."

"I can only see them when I've taken something."

The other woman nodded. "That isn't uncommon. Why do you ask?"

"I saw my mother. I don't know why or how."

"And it's been days." Miss Woodward gave her a level look. "It's only natural for them to seek out their loved ones. You were especially receptive then." She paused. "Is that why you rushed out of the dance?"

"Part of it." Laurel bit her lip. "I guess I want to be normal. I don't know what Mr. Masters must be thinking."

"Did you tell him?"

"No."

"Do you intend to marry him?"

Laurel's eyes widened. "How did you…?"

"He looks like he's won a prestigious award when he looks at you."

"I don't know. Should I? I mean, he is rather nice."

"'Rather nice' isn't marriage ready. 'Rather nice' is the neighbor you borrow sugar from or who opens the door for you. Unless your feelings change, I say to hell with 'father nice.'"

Laurel caught a giggle behind her hand. "When you put it that way…"

"As I was saying, unless you intend to marry him, it doesn't matter what he thinks of you. Is it strange to see ghosts? Only to those who haven't."

"Why are you being so nice to me?"

Those brilliant blue eyes took in her face. "You're a friend of my cousin's from what I'm told."

"Not according to my father. I'm not even sure I should be talking to you."

"Aw, yes. The Woodward name strikes again. Don't worry, our conversation will be our secret."

"I'm sorry."

"Don't be. I'm used to it."

Laurel squared her shoulders. "You shouldn't have to be." If only she could make her father understand that the Woodwards weren't all bad. Surely, Miss Woodward's actions toward her tonight had proven as much, and Conner's generosity and caring had gone a long way to convince her as well.

"Don't get yourself in trouble because of me, or for Conner, for that matter. Family is more important than anything."

"I'll have you know, I will get into trouble for whomever I please."

Miss Woodward laughed.

Laurel dropped her shoulders. "Though you're right, it will have to be our secret. At least, for now." She didn't know what she planned to do, but she was tired of her father choosing her friends. It was a good thing he approved of Maya, though not from having known her very well. He wasn't normally so overbearing, but when it came to the Woodwards, it was personal.

She would make him explain the truth. The whole story of why the Woodwards were considered so horrible. Yes, casting out tenants behind on their rent was horrible, but understandable. How else were the Woodwards supposed to make a living?

She knew she was making excuses for them, but she couldn't help it. She had grown fond of Miss Woodward regardless of what Maya presumed, and Conner had always been a good but distant friend.

Could it be something about Lord Tenwich?

"You know, he cares about you."

Laurel caught her gaze. "What?"

Miss Woodward chuckled. "I know it doesn't seem like it, but you're all he talks about."

"It doesn't matter." Laurel looked away.

"I know. The old goat would never allow it."

"My father?"

"Lord Tenwich, but your father too. It's a shame. You make a sweet couple, but it doesn't mean you can't be friends."

"No, it does."

"I see." Miss Woodward stared off. "Well, our secret conversation won't be so secret after all."

Maya marched onto the terrace, fire in her eyes. "Are you trying to steal my best friend from me? Or are you plotting murder?" She regarded Miss Woodward.

Miss Woodward gave her a small smile. "Neither. I'm glad we had this talk." She patted Laurel on the shoulder.

Miss Woodward excused herself and Maya faced Laurel. "What talk?"

"Ghosts." She wasn't lying but omitting what Maya wanted to hear. She didn't need any more pressure to defy her father.

Maya shook her head. "People are starting to miss you."

She thought of Mr. Masters and her heart tripped. "He must think I'm the worst creature."

Maya gave her a reassuring smile. "Of course, he doesn't. He asked your father for an audience tomorrow."

"Oh, dear." Laurel swallowed.

"I suggest you make up your mind about what you want because you can't have it all. As much as I love you, you're getting rather tedious."

"Do you hate me?"

Maya poked her in the ribs. "No, I don't hate you. You little fool, I said I love you, but you need to stop giving me a headache with all this turnaround. Marry Mr. Masters. Become a nun. Just let me know what you decide."

Laurel sighed. She thought she already decided when she rushed out onto the terrace, but could she live with her decision? Could she defy her family's wishes for her to gain her own happiness? Surely, Mr. Masters would be miserable with an unloving wife.

When it came down to it, she didn't have a choice. Her heart wouldn't let her.

Maya and Laurel returned to the ballroom. A wide smile drew up on Laurel's lips, creasing her eyes. Now that her decision was made, nothing could bring down her mood, not even the man making his way toward her.

The flickering candlelight emphasized the waves in his hair and the resemblance between him and Miss Woodward was striking. They had similar angular bone structure and coloring, though Miss Woodward was paler and carried herself with more grace.

Laurel stopped and Maya gave her a wide smile before leaving her to welcome the man Laurel would have to refuse.

"I know I shouldn't be talking to you, but I couldn't help myself." He bowed before her and kissed her gloved hand. "Are you angry with me?"

Gooseflesh rose along her arms, and she shivered.

"I can't avoid you forever."

"You can't?" The edge of his mouth curled up.

"It's impossible." Even as she sensed her father's gaze on her, she couldn't help but draw closer to the man. It was senseless but what else could she do? She couldn't be rude.

"I'm glad I've made that impression on you."

Her hands shook. He was referring to their time in the study. Warmth flooded between her legs as she remembered the stroke of his tongue. "Not here."

"Where then?"

She shook her head, but she couldn't hold back her smile.

"Come dance with me."

She hesitated.

"It's a country dance. Nothing scandalous about it."

Laurel had already had her scandalous moments with him at the festival, but she didn't need to exercise the consequences further. As much as she needed to refuse, it would be the height of rude unless she wanted to sit the rest of the dance out.

She trod a thin line with her father, but he couldn't deny she had to abide by propriety. The Woodwards were an important family, and it was unheard of to shun them. At least, that is what she told herself as she allowed Conner to lead her to the dance floor.

Few words passed between them as they carried through with the steps, but their gazes never strayed from each other. She tried to hold on to her anger at him and clutched wildly for her devotion to her father, but their argument before seemed to melt away and it was as though nothing had happened.

Her reasons against spending time with Conner were hollow once they exchanged bows at the close of the music. They stood facing each other until the musicians struck the next chord and they were forced to either dance or join the sidelines. So, they danced.

It was the Harvest Festival all over again. They danced with the same mirth and cared little for their craft, though they took the steps with admirable skill. Only a breath of time existed until the second dance concluded, but there wouldn't be a third.

Her father collected her from the dance floor. No longer did he wait to see the antics of his youngest daughter. Allie took up her other arm as they made their excuses and left into the chill night air.

"What are you doing? I wasn't finished." Laurel pulled her arms away.

Her father faced her. "Yes, you were. How can you embarrass us in front of everyone?"

"Embarrass you? You embarrass yourself. I couldn't refuse to dance with him not if I wanted to enjoy the rest of the night."

Her father waved this away. "Then you won't dance the rest of the night. How hard can that be?"

Allie cleared her throat. "Father, you remember what it was like."

Their father regarded her with wide eyes.

"No, I suppose not." Her sister sighed. "Laurel, one dance is fine, but did you really have to dance with him twice?"

Yes, she started to say. "I didn't want to appear rude."

Her father made a choking sound. "Not from where I stood."

Laurel joined her arm with her sister's and set out down the road. Besides the autumn chill, it was a nice night, and the Atwells had walked from their home. It all seemed long ago and the prospect of talking to her father the entire way home made her stomach lurch.

Their father easily caught up with them and took Laurel's other side. "I don't think you understand the enormity of what you've done."

Laurel kept her gaze glued forward.

"I didn't think I had to explain to you my reasons, but I guess I was wrong. Obeying your father shouldn't be optional." He hesitated as though he were gathering his words. "Allie is not your mother's first child."

Laurel nodded. "She miscarried."

"That's true, but she didn't tell you it was not my child."

Allie and Laurel halted in the middle of the road with matching wide-eyed stares.

He nodded. "It's true. She was with child when we married."

"She was pregnant with another man's child, and you married her anyway?" Laurel's chest tightened.

"It was the right thing to do. She would have been ruined."

She knew her father was a good man, but this was above and beyond her understanding of him. "I thought it was a love match."

"Don't get me wrong. I was in love with your mother. It wasn't her fault."

"She was the one who got pregnant."

"Against her will. You see, your mother worked as a maid at Tenwich House for years before we were married."

Laurel's face paled. "You mean to tell me that the child was Lord Tenwich's?"

He sighed. "You wouldn't think it of him, but he has a certain way with his employees."

"Bastard." Laurel clenched her fists.

"Normally, I would correct your language, but I have to agree." Allie shook her head.

Laurel's voice softened. "What happened?"

"The same thing that happened to all the pregnant maids. She was let go and forced to return to your grandparents."

"He didn't even try to claim the child?"

"Listen, Laurel, this is how the Woodwards work. They care nothing for the people they trample on to get what they want. The same goes for Conner Woodward."

She gritted her teeth. Conner had taken advantage of her when she was vulnerable though she had allowed his attentions. That didn't mean he wasn't the same as his father. She couldn't imagine what it was like to be an employee there. The opportunity to harass the maids was too great. How could the Woodwards resist?

He was careful. She would give him that much. He was waiting for the perfect moment. Why else would he renew their friendship? She wasn't suited for marriage, and few would care if the odd Tenwich girl was ruined. He wanted her, but not for the reasons she dreamed.

She took a deep breath. "You're right, father. Conner Woodward is trouble. I'll stop seeing him." And someday soon, she would give the Woodwards exactly what they deserve.

Chapter 21

Her ties cut with Conner and her refusal of Mr. Masters's suit, Laurel was unburdened and listless the following day. Her curiosity, however, was as active as a night roaming cat. With her father's insistence, she was past ready to give up the missing corpses, but she couldn't bring herself to forget seeing her mother with the witches.

Her last and most undesirable option was Sally Reed. She had sent word to Maya to try to convince Miss Reed to visit her since Laurel wouldn't leave the house for fear of running into Conner, and shortly after noon, Maya had sent word that Miss Reed would accompany her to the Atwells.

After two in the afternoon, Laurel hid away her mending as her friend and her enemy strolled into the parlor. Maya took the seat next to Laurel. Sally Reed looked down her nose at Laurel, made a sound in the back of her mouth, and sat across from the pair.

The seat Miss Reed had chosen was a well-sprung, upholstered number, but as soon as she sat down, she squirmed in discomfort. Luckily, the woman didn't say anything, but her complaint was clear. Laurel felt the criticism like a sticky weed and tried not to show her humiliation.

She stared Miss Reed down. "Good afternoon, Miss Reed. Miss Meadows." She sent her smile into her voice.

"Hmm," Miss Reed said.

"I suppose Miss Meadows told you why I wanted to speak with you?"

Miss Reed eyed her. "In part." She flexed her wrist. "Something about witches."

Laurel nodded. "I'd like to know more about the Tenwich witches."

"I don't know what there is to tell." Miss Reed frowned.

Maya gave her a half-smile. If Laurel was going to get any answers, she might as well get straight to the matter at hand.

"Miss Reed, what was the ritual for? And what was the smoke?"

Miss Reed shifted in her chair and sighed as though she would never find any comfort. "We celebrate the harvest. It's just an extension of the Harvest Festival."

"And the smoke?"

Her dark eyes narrowed. "I believe we used rosemary and sage."

Laurel leaned forward. "Is it common for people to see ghosts?"

Miss Reed shook her brunette head. "I've never seen them but during that ritual, I'm not surprised."

"Why is that?"

"Because, Miss Atwell, we were putting the dead to rest."

Laurel's head jerked to face Miss Reed. "Then you admit you have something to do with the stolen corpses."

"Goodness, no. We were settling the ghosts into peace. We do it every full moon since the bodies started to disappear. The ghosts of the dead tend to wander when you disturb their bodies. Who did you see?" Miss Reed raised a brow in her pointed face.

Laurel swallowed. "My mother."

Miss Reed nodded. "You can be assured that she is at peace now. I'm sorry you had to go through that."

Perhaps Miss Reed did have a heart.

"Thank you." Laurel gave her a small smile.

Miss Reed cast her gaze away and waved a hand. "We do it for everyone whose body is taken. At least, those we are aware of. I do wish they would stop."

"It's horrible." Maya's voice was hoarse.

"It's exhausting is what it is. Full moon rituals used to be fun. Now they're filled with death and misery."

Maya and Laurel exchanged looks.

"Do you have any idea who is taking the bodies?" Laurel asked.

"If I did, we would have stopped this madness, and I wouldn't be here," Miss Reed spat out. She reminded Laurel of a snake that spits venom, except Miss Reed's words were the venom, and she used them to slowly kill her foes.

"What about a black dog? Did you see any?"

Miss Reed pulled back as though Laurel had struck her. "What are you playing at? Of course, I haven't seen a black dog. I don't know what you've gotten yourself into, but you should stop before someone gets hurt. This is Conner Woodward's influence, isn't it? You need to stay away from him. His family is cursed, and so is anyone else who gets in their path."

Cursed? What nonsense was she spewing now?

"I assure you, I have nothing more to do with that man." Nor did she intend to have anything else to do with his family.

Miss Reed shot to her feet and smoothed her skirts. "I need to go." She marched to the door before the rest of them could rise. "You're seeing demon dogs. Watch your back."

The door shut behind her and Laurel fell back into the seat she had just vacated.

"That was interesting," Maya said from her side.

"Interesting?" Laurel snorted. "At least now I know what the witches were doing. They seemed harmless to me."

Maya nodded. "Oh, they are. Only don't tell the Reverend. He wouldn't be pleased."

"To say the least." Laurel stretched out her legs and relaxed back in her chair.

"Have you decided to stop seeing Conner?"

"I'm afraid I have to. As much as I'm attracted to him, he's a bad match for me. I'm afraid he brings out the worst in me."

"But he makes you happy."

"You know I obey every word of my father."

Maya shrugged. "When it suits you."

Laurel glared at her. "Every word, but when it comes to Conner, I find myself going off on my own more and more."

Maya nudged her with an elbow. "You're growing up. That isn't such a bad thing."

"Maya, I'm losing the battle. I need to do as my father says. He knows what's best for me."

"Is Mr. Masters what's best for you?"

Laurel shook her head. "I don't know what is, but I would be miserable with him."

"How can anyone be miserable with those

dimples? Sally must be right, you've lost your mind."

Laurel laughed with her friend. "Perhaps you have another man in mind for me? Someone…less perfect."

Maya blinked. "Less perfect?" She chuckled. "I'll do what I can."

"Thank you. You're a great friend to me."

"And don't forget it. You owe me. The last thing I wanted to do was spend an afternoon with Sally Reed."

"I thought you were friends."

"Me? Friends with her? That's laughable. She only tolerates me because of my connections."

"Then why did she come?"

"She was curious. The same reason people tour madhouses."

"That's rather blunt."

"You wanted the truth. If it's any consolation, I don't think you're mad. Perhaps you're a bit odd but nothing that I would lock away in the attic."

"I still don't know what happened with the bodies, and why do I have a demon dog following me?"

"I'd say you should ask Conner again. I've heard he's making a lot of calls."

Laurel shot her a dark look.

Maya raised her hands. "I know. I know. I'll see myself out. I still have another call to make before dinner."

Laurel ignored her friend as she left and pulled out her mending basket. She needed a steady mind and sewing the next shroud would keep her level. If she could believe Sally Reed, the witches were beneficial. At least now she could find some closure with her mother.

Demon dogs and missing bodies. They had to be

connected.

She wouldn't consult Conner. She would have to find some other source of information, and she couldn't get it from the graveyard. Unless... no, it was too crazy. Her father was on the mend, but would he possibly accompany her? Conner wouldn't dare approach her with her father present.

She could always try sneaking out again. Conner couldn't be there all the time. Something clicked in her mind that hadn't occurred to her before. Mr. Masters had said Conner could communicate with the dead. Couldn't that mean that when under the influence of herbs or absinthe she could too?

If anyone knew where the bodies were being taken, it was the dead, but wouldn't the witches have tried? Probably not if they were anything like Sally Reed. They wouldn't have access to the ghosts if they couldn't see them. Yet, Miss Woodward had said anyone could see ghosts. Who was correct?

She supposed it wouldn't hurt to try. She would have to disobey her father one last time. He would understand if she could explain it to him, but she wouldn't try until after the fact, or rather until she was caught.

Her father and Allie were in the workshop as usual. It was the perfect time to do something stupid.

Laurel set to work, moving off to the kitchen and the stashes of bottled herbs. She found the rosemary and sage which they used for cooking and found a ceramic bowl. She crushed the herbs, allowing the pine-like scents to fill her nostrils.

The hearth held embers from the afternoon meal and Laurel was able to capture a small flame which she introduced to the herbs.

The fire was small and needed constant encouragement, but the resulting smoke filled her head with a sharp drowning sensation. She continued to burn the herbs until there was nothing but a sooty residue in the bowl. Then, she waited.

It wasn't long before a paw clawed at her skirts.

She smiled down at Rollo and bent to pat him on the head. This time, the tangled fur pressed into her palm.

She shook her head.

Laurel doubted she would ever get used to the difference or understand whether or not she could touch an apparition. Maybe it depended on how much of the herb or the absinthe was in her. If either absinthe or the herbs worked, how?

A void occupied her chest. She wished Conner was here to ask, but with her luck, he probably didn't know the answers either. It seemed the more she figured out, the more questions arose. At least now she had a way of getting her questions answered. Of course, Conner had said there weren't many ghosts in the graveyard, but she had to try.

She donned her jacket, tied her bonnet, and slipped out the kitchen door. The wind struck her with a sharp, blustering force, sending the gentle tinkle of the chimes on the side of the house into a high-pitched clatter.

Laurel pulled the jacket around her and wished she had grabbed a shawl, but she had already taken the next step and she didn't want to take the chance someone would walk into the house as she left. She doubted her luck would hold out that long.

The trees whipped and shuttered around her as she

traversed the trail to the graveyard. Nothing met her but the burst of wind upon her face. She held her bonnet still as she crossed the graveyard when a shape moved among the markers.

At this point, she hadn't seen anyone, ghost or otherwise. The graveyard was, well, dead. The shape moved with a determined stride, and it took her a moment to realize it was the shape of a large canine. The demon dog.

She stiffened and took a step back.

This was what she wanted. She had to find out what had become of the bodies, and maybe if she got close enough, she could communicate with it the same way she had with Rollo. It was a bit of a stretch, but she didn't see any other ghosts here.

Rollo growled beside her, and she frowned.

"You stay here," she commanded the ghost dog.

Rollo whined.

"I know, but I have to do this. I don't know what that thing will do to you, and I'd rather not find out."

The dog dropped to a sitting position.

"Good boy."

Laurel took a deep breath and stepped closer to the demon dog. Each step wasn't any easier than the first, but she managed to follow the dog into the churchyard without it paying her any mind.

The shape seemed to be searching for something, but what she didn't know. She followed it as it sniffed the air, stopping and starting at odd locations. They exited the churchyard and found the road leading to the church. The dog perked up its ears and pointed down the road, shooting into a run.

Laurel ran after the apparition. Her side hitched as

they leaped down the road. They made it to the outskirts of town to the road leading out of Tenwich. There at the adjoining streets, the dog stopped.

She closed the distance between them, and at last, the demon dog regarded her.

Her stomach was in her throat as it examined her.

Its eyes appeared the size of saucers and its dark coat seemed to shimmer like light on water. It was beyond the size of a large dog, but something near a small horse. It sniffed the air between them, and gooseflesh rose on her arms and neck. The apparition sneezed before turning its attention back to the ground.

It made a noise between a cry and a growl and pawed at the ground at the crossroads.

She near jumped out of her skin at the sound. "What is it?"

The dog tilted its head to the side, studying her once again. Every hair on her body seemed to stand on end. A long minute passed. Then, it started to dig.

Her eyes widened as the hole deepened—until, at last, the outline of a skeletal finger and the hand it was attached to came into view.

Chapter 22

The services were unlike any Laurel had witnessed before. The bodies of seven people were reburied in their proper places. Two of which they had no idea were missing from their graves. Most of the people of Tenwich turned out to give the deceased a sendoff once again.

The Reverend did an admirable job including all the deceased, remembering anecdotes from years ago that would otherwise be forgotten. The citizens of Tenwich crowded around the graves, each at a time while they mourned their losses once again.

When it came to Laurel's mother, the silence over the graveyard increased the hollow sensation in her chest. Her mother had been one of the first corpses to be found at the crossroads, and ever since, Laurel had gone numb. It was as though her mother had died a second time, as the services suggested.

Whoever had dug up the bodies and buried them at the crossroads had a warped sense of righteousness. In the past, those who had died by their own hand would be buried at the crossroads. In this case, the suicides were either direct or indirect.

The mayor had died of alcohol. The man had drunk himself to death each night until his body couldn't handle the strain anymore, but he was only one of the seven. Another deceased, Miss Bates, had died in an attempt to end her pregnancy with the aid of potions from a doctor. The procedure had failed, and Miss Bates had died from the poison put in her body.

Laurel's mother had ended her own life.

Her mother's mind had been drifting for years to the point she couldn't care for herself. Her father, Laurel, and Allie all took turns caring for her until ultimately Laurel took over. The end had come as a relief and a day of great loss. It was as though she had fallen into quicksand that sucked her to the bottom of an ever-growing void.

The scene she had walked in on was like no other. Her mother had taken the rest of the laudanum they had set aside for small doses. The guilt of leaving her mother alone with the bottle had eaten away at her ever since.

When she entered, her mother's eyes were glass-like, and her mother wasn't quite asleep, but also not awake. The breath had fled from her mother's body and with it, something intangible. She was gone.

Laurel had lost the comforting presence of her mother, and she had gained a freedom she would gladly trade to have her mother back if only for one last conversation, one last hug, or one last laugh.

As though on cue, the sun peeked out of the gray clouds after their last memorial. Laurel let the warmth play over her face as she closed her eyes.

"I'm sorry about your mother. I don't know if I ever told you."

Laurel's eyes snapped open to Sally Reed beside her. "Thank you."

"She would be proud of you."

Laurel cocked her head. "How so?" As far as she

knew, she hadn't accomplished anything her mother would be proud of.

"You escaped the Woodward family in time, which was something she had failed to do."

She stiffened. "What happened?"

"I'm not sure I should discuss it."

Laurel almost laughed. There was nothing Miss Reed wouldn't gossip about. Perhaps the woman cared what Laurel thought of her. Unlikely.

She gave her a small smile. "It's all right. We're friends here."

Miss Reed sniffed. "Another maid was dismissed."

"Was she…?"

Miss Reed nodded. "Three months along. She had tried to hide it. Mr. Woodward sent her off. Now, she's without a home or prospects. The poor girl."

"Mr. Woodward? You mean Lord Tenwich."

"No, Mr. Conner Woodward. You can ask around, but I think you know I'm telling the truth. He's bad news, Miss Atwell. You saved yourself from ruin."

"Conner?" Her lips framed the word, but she wasn't sure if any sound came out. She couldn't believe it of him, but was it so much of a stretch? Sons often repeated the transgressions of their fathers. "Where is the girl now?"

"She was here for the services. I don't know where she went off to."

Everyone had been there for the services, all save the Woodwards and Lady Quinn. Women weren't normally meant to witness such gatherings, but the enormity of the event had pushed the boundaries of propriety. The Reverend couldn't deny that.

"You have to be wrong. Who did you hear this

from?"

Miss Reed's eyes snapped wide. "My maid."

It was gossip. That was the only explanation. She tried to push the information from her mind, but it hung there like a dangling carrot for a horse. Her heart ached for the maid, but what did she care what Conner Woodward did?

"If it makes it any easier, ask her for yourself. Her name is Miss Tawny Lowe. Find out where she is staying, and you'll have your answers." Miss Reed gave her a nod and sauntered off over the lawn.

She shouldn't care whether Conner Woodward was as evil as Miss Reed indicated. She had nothing to do with the man anymore. He was none of her concern, and yet, she couldn't help searching the dispersing crowd for any signs of a woman matching Miss Reed's description.

A pregnant maid could only go to so many places in Tenwich, but Laurel had a feeling she knew which one, and she would be damned if she was caught at the brothel. She would have to take Miss Reed's word for it. Conner Woodward was as bad, no, worse than his father. It took a special kind of evil to commit the same atrocities as your father when viewed in retrospect.

Laurel found her father and Allie standing over her mother's grave for one last moment, and they walked back together in silence. The sun had stayed out for a change and the weather kept the way it had during the summer. Sadness was foreign on days like today, but here they were.

Without a word, Allie prepared their afternoon meal. There was enough bread and cheese for a quick bite before they returned to the workshop and Laurel returned to her mending. Most of Tenwich had declared a time for mourning, but the Atwells had no such luxury. Laurel had a new basket to work through, and the dead didn't wait on the living.

There was still the question of who had taken the bodies and killed Mr. Boswell, but right now, all Laurel could think of was Conner and how she had misjudged his character. The betrayal crumbled her heart into a little ball and smashed it against the wall.

She had let him in and allowed him into her most secret moments. Not only that, but she had also cared for him in a way she hadn't cared for another person. All previous talk had gone over her head, but this news from Miss Reed stank like trash in the summer.

To think she had considered Maya's advice to sleep with him. She should feel relief, but instead, that numb sensation she had acquired after finding her mother's corpse had grown and strengthened. She doubted she would feel anything if Allie took a hammer to her head.

The news from Sally Reed opened up new possibilities into Conner's character. How many times had he taken advantage of his employees? If he didn't have any scruples about such things, what other atrocities had he committed?

She pictured a long train of unmarried women coming from Tenwich House, all destitute and hopeless. Without her family, she might have joined that group. She couldn't imagine starting a new life without the support of her family, and many of those women, no doubt, were.

Laurel wished she could cry, or better yet, scream. All the injustice in the world couldn't bring a response from her body. It was as though she were one of the dead recovered from the graves at the crossroads. Maybe they should have buried her in the graveyard too.

Before she could dig herself a deeper hole with her grief, a knock came at the door. A note of surprise tickled her consciousness as she recognized Mr. Masters. Without a chaperone, they shouldn't be alone, but at the time, Laurel couldn't find the energy to care, and she greeted him without enthusiasm.

They settled in chairs across from each other near the window where she had set down her mending. The parlor was dark for the time of day, and the window had helped with her work without wasting a candle.

"I meant to visit you after the services. It must have been hard on you."

She nodded, trying to keep her attention on his features but failing. "Thank you." Her voice was barely audible.

"I don't know the customs of mourning or if you need to begin again." He paused, waiting to see if she would respond. "I would like to try again."

Laurel mustered a small smile.

"We can see how our relationship goes and, in the future, I will discuss with you whether or not you want me to speak with your father."

"All right." What choice did she have now? He was as good a husband as any man.

"I would like to take you driving if you're up to it."

She gave a short nod.

"Does today suit you?"

Laurel glanced at her mending and peered back at the door leading to the workshop. "Better make it tomorrow. I can have Allie accompany me."

He cleared his throat. "Right." He glanced around the room as though searching for something. "I hope I'm not intruding."

She wanted to reassure him, but she didn't like to lie. "It is always a pleasure to see you."

The moments ticked by, and the air seemed to fizzle with awkwardness, but she couldn't bring herself to show him the door. Though she didn't want to marry him, Mr. Masters was a kind man, and she remembered such kindness and returned it. The least she could do was give him her time.

An audience with Mr. Masters was far different without Allie's presence. The couple had little in common, and once again, she wondered why he wanted a match with her. He could do far better with a relation like Lady Quinn.

"Why do you court me?" she blurted out.

He tapped his hat on his crossed leg as though in thought. He smiled and then his smile dropped. "You'll think I'm silly."

She shook her head. "Believe me. I've heard a lot of nonsense lately and I doubt it could be any sillier than what I've been through."

His eyes brightened. "Yes, well, I have this dream of what I want in a wife. When I return home, when I wake up in the morning, or when I sit at the dinner table, I want to feel the love of a woman through her smile. I want her to glow, to laugh. I want someone who will share the joys of life with me the ways so few do."

"And you think I'm that woman?"

"Exactly. The way you look at the world, the way

you blossom when you're happy. I want that in my life."

She sighed. "I'm not happy."

"Yes, I know, but somehow, you have shown me how to experience life even when you are your saddest. I saw you happy at the Harvest Festival and then with Maya. Yet, in your sadness, the depth of your feeling is extraordinary. You live like no other woman I have encountered."

"You must not have met many women. I've spent most of my hours in the graveyard or helping my mother. I'm surrounded by death."

He shook his head. "In death is where we find life. It is fleeting."

She let out a long breath. "You've given me much to think about."

He stood, catching her cue. "You will consider my offer?"

Her smile reached her eyes. "Yes, and I look forward to tomorrow."

He beamed back at her. "Then I take my leave of you." He bowed and let himself out of the door.

She stared after him a moment, wondering what had transpired. The man was far different from what she was used to with Conner. It was no wonder she couldn't place him. He was like a foreign prince imposing his strange views on new land. Marriage with him would be full of surprises, if nothing else.

Marriage or not, her future didn't quite seem so dismal after all. Who was to say happiness was defined by the person one married? She would define her own life and set her own terms for her happiness.

Did she want to marry Mr. Masters? She didn't

know any more than she had before, but what she did know was she couldn't base her happiness on her family's needs but rather on her own abilities to cultivate a happy life.

She pushed aside her mending and steeled her spine. She would talk with her father. It was time they addressed the situation of her lack of a partner once again. As promising as Mr. Masters was, she would rather not place their wellbeing in his hands.

Chapter 23

Sawdust floated about the workshop, hitting rays of sunlight from the windows. The air was dry here and left a papery taste in Laurel's mouth. Her nostrils were filled with the dust of the cabinetry profession, and it took every ounce of her willpower to keep herself there.

One look at Allie and Mr. Cross and they both fled the workshop. It was rare for Laurel to visit them, so they must have deemed it important enough to take a break while Laurel spoke to her father.

Her father stopped his hammering long enough to acknowledge her, then he completed his task and set down the hammer.

"I didn't want to interrupt you but it's important."

Her father wiped a hand over his brow.

"You were right about Conner."

He started to speak but she raised a hand to stop him.

"Mr. Masters wants to try again. I'm not sure what I want to do but I'd like to give him a chance. I don't know if it's the best thing for me, or even if marriage is. I need to find that out for myself."

"Of course, marriage is right for you. You would be a fool to refuse Mr. Masters a second time."

"I want to do what will make me happy and not what will make you happy."

"My dear, we need you to marry. We can't support

you forever."

Laurel took a deep breath. "If it comes down to it, I will find a way to support myself. If Allie can do it, so can I."

"There's a difference. Allie is getting married."

"You're right. I'm not Allie. Unlike her, I would make an excellent governess."

"A governess in Tenwich." He shook his head. "Few can afford such a luxury."

She rolled her shoulders back. "Then I will move to town, but I'm not going to marry because it is expected of me. I can do this."

He gave her a hard stare. "I wish I had the confidence you do, but it's a hard world out there, especially for young women."

Her hands clenched into fists. "Don't you see? I would rather be destitute than living in an unhappy marriage."

"Don't be foolish."

"It isn't foolish. Besides, if things go well with Mr. Masters, then this conversation will be for naught. He's a good man, father, better than I thought he was."

"I thought so."

"That doesn't mean he's right for me. I want someone who will fill me with warmth."

Someone to light a fire underneath her that drives her forward through life, instead of dragging her along. She wanted someone who would encourage her to be a better version of herself and not tolerate her often melancholy moods so much like her mother's. Her husband should be supportive but not only financially. They would be a team against the woes of the world.

In essence, she didn't want to marry a man like her

father. He meant well and he worked hard, but he wasn't the husband her mother had needed. Her death wasn't anyone's fault, but their marriage hadn't helped either.

"Don't be such a child."

"I'm not being a child. It's time I grew up, and that means taking responsibility for my future. I can do this."

"You say that but do you even know what you're getting yourself into? You're meant to run a household and you can't even prepare a meal."

She raised her chin. "Yes, I can. I've run the house since mother was confined. True, Allie took care of the cooking, but I did everything else. Who do you think mended and washed your clothes? Or scrubbed down the floors? Who do you think called for the doctor when mother needed it? I ran the household while you were in the workshop."

"That isn't the same."

She folded her arms over her chest. "It may not seem like it, but I was taking the responsibility off of your hands. Allie cooked and worked with you. I did everything else."

"If you take this path, you'll be more miserable than if you land in a loveless marriage."

"You don't know that. You can't. You married for love, remember?"

His jaw was set in a hard line, but he didn't respond.

She nodded. "How happy do you think you would be if you hadn't had Mother?"

"I had a profession. A shop."

"Which you purchased with mother's dowry."

Her father's face reddened. "You have no right to come in here and lecture me when you're the one who needs to find a husband. Go off. Do what you want but get out of my sight. I don't want to hear another word from you until you have come to your senses. Marriage is your best option, and you know it."

Laurel huffed and marched from the workshop and came into the kitchen where Allie and Mr. Cross sat nibbling on biscuits. The air was thick with heat, and she started to sweat the moment she stepped over the threshold.

"Are you all right?" Allie asked.

Mr. Cross kept his head down, most likely not wanting to get involved.

"No. I'm not."

Her sister smiled. "You will be." She patted Laurel's arm but was rebuffed.

"How can you be so sure about everything? Why won't you let us understand?"

Allie shook her head. "It isn't something you can understand, but something you are. I can't explain it. It just is. Mother was better at this sort of thing."

"She didn't seem so sure about the future."

Allie sighed. "Yes, she was. She knew what was waiting for her, and she used the last bit of her mind to save us from it, but she also knew we would be well without her."

"It doesn't feel right."

Allie refused Laurel's protests and draped an arm around her shoulders. "It doesn't, but your time is coming. You just need to be patient."

"Is it Mr. Masters?"

Her sister shook her head. "I can't tell you that."

"Can't or won't?"

"I don't know. I only know that you're headed to the most important decision of your life, but whatever you choose, it will come out the way it needs to be."

"That doesn't make sense."

Mr. Cross chuckled. "She rarely does."

Allie glanced at him from the corner of her eyes. "Laurel, why don't you take a walk? Clear your head. I promise it will help."

"I'm not supposed to walk in the graveyard."

"Who's going to know? Father is busy fuming, and we certainly are unaware of it. Aren't we, Mr. Cross?"

He smiled, making him appear boyish and younger than his twenty-six years. Laurel could see what Allie saw in him at that moment. He would make an excellent brother.

Laurel laughed, though the sound was hollow. She didn't have much enthusiasm for a walk, but she would do it anyway. Allie must be trying to get rid of her so she could spend time with Mr. Cross.

She blinked away the sun as she set out from the kitchen door. She wanted to go back to bed, curl up around a book, and forget the world. Her conversation with her father did nothing to reassure her about her choices, but she planned to stick it out until her plans bore fruit.

Leaves crunched and swept from under her boots, and she kicked the offending barriers as she went. Autumn had landed over Tenwich, and winter was fast approaching. Already the crisp bite of air required a shawl, which she had grabbed before she left the comfort of home.

All that was needed was the glint of the sun off

fallen snow. They were halfway there, though it was now October and it seemed only days had passed since the heat of the sun had brought sweat down her spine.

She murmured her usual greetings to the graves, but this time she wondered if the ghosts of the deceased were listening, though she knew it was unlikely. Yet, they had buried the missing corpses this morning, and she wondered if that would put them at rest or if they would wait for the witches.

The moon was full that day, and she intended to investigate the forest that night, but this time she would be prepared with the help of the sage and rosemary she had used before. No point relying on others for the effects of the smoke.

Her speed picked up as she passed the Woodward crypt, but she only managed to make more noise. She winced as the door of the crypt creaked open, revealing the man she had tried to avoid.

Conner studied her with a glint in his eyes that created a silvery cast to them. His hair and clothes were messed as though he had slept in the crypt, and he had only now risen. She wanted to laugh at the thought of him rising from the dead, but the serious set of his jaw left her silent.

They stared each other down until Laurel spun on her heel and sped away.

"Laurel, stop."

Her shoulders snapped to her ears. "Don't you dare call me that."

"Whatever it is I've done, I'm sorry."

"That's no way to start an apology." She started off again, but her skirts hindered her pace.

"Wait. I deserve an explanation."

She rounded on him. "You deserve nothing from me. What we did was the worst idea imaginable."

"You didn't seem to think so."

She raised a hand. "It was a momentary lapse in judgment. You took advantage of me."

"We've had this conversation before. You know I wouldn't do anything like that."

"Do I?"

"You should." He folded his arms.

"And just how should I know? You treat women as though they are your playthings, just as your father."

"I am nothing like my father."

"Prove it. Walk away from me and never speak to me again."

He lowered his brows. "How does that prove anything?"

She closed her eyes. "If you cared for me, even a small amount, you would leave me be. I need to live my life."

"That's backward."

She averted her gaze. "Fine. Just leave me alone."

"But why? What have I done to you that's so horrible?"

"It isn't what you've done to me but what you do to the people in Tenwich. I can't be seen with you, and I certainly can't entertain a friendship with you. You and your father are like poison to the people here." She shook her head. "I need to protect myself."

He flinched. "If this is about the Boswells, they were given six months. I don't know what else I could have done."

"What about Miss Tawny Lowe?"

"What about her?"

Shrouds

"Did you dismiss her from your household?"

"Yes." He hurried on as she turned back away. "I had to. My father wouldn't tolerate her in our employ, but I gave her a generous severance."

A solid weight landed on her chest, and she gripped her shirt over the area. "How could you do such a thing?"

He squinted. "It happens all the time."

Her mouth fell open in disbelief. She walked away before he could say any more. This time, she didn't stop when he called out to her, and he didn't try to catch up to her. In her haste. *Good. Let him learn something from her disgust.*

How could she be so stupid? Of course, he was just like his father, and she was foolish like her mother. Only the good sense she had inherited from her father had saved her from the same fate as the Woodward employees.

That poor woman, and he had given her money as though a child could be bought off. The maid needed more than a heavy purse to get through single motherhood. She would need work and a place to stay, two things that Conner had taken from her. The child would need a father, but that would be too much to ask of the Woodwards.

She clenched her fists. She had made a mistake defending him in the past, and her previous decision to sever ties with him had been right. The realization only soured her stomach and sent bile up her throat.

How many women were homeless and without options because of Conner or his father? How many women would it take for Conner to be so callous about his actions? It was a number Laurel couldn't imagine any human being could count.

She shook her head and clutched her shawl closer. The cold had deepened. She needed to go home, but she couldn't face Allie and her father right now. She couldn't go back to the graveyard where she usually sought solace, and there was only one other place she could think of.

Maya wouldn't judge her choices, and it was long overdue that she brought her friend up to speed. She had only seen a brief glimpse of her friend at the services, but it was enough to know the effect of the funerals on her had been enough to send her home without visitors. At least, visitors who weren't Laurel.

Together, the two women could share battle stories with the men they had banished from their lives. She would leave it to Maya to find humor in the situation. A good cry alone with her best friend would do wonders for her, or at least that is what she had planned.

What she found at Maya's was the opposite of what she had imagined.

Chapter 24

The last person Laurel expected to see at Maya's house was Miss Amelia Woodward. The dark-haired beauty sat straight on the edge of one of Maya's favorite red damask chairs. Her resemblance to her cousin sent a chill along Laurel's spine.

"Miss Woodward, I didn't know you would be calling," Laurel said.

"Miss Meadows and I got a poor start to our relationship. I thought it prudent to remedy that. Please, Miss Atwell, call me Amelia."

Laurel didn't reciprocate the favor. She wanted nothing to do with the Woodwards and that included Miss Woodward.

Her gaze shifted between the women and Maya gave her a false smile and gestured for her to take a seat in the other red damask chair while Maya occupied the adjacent sofa. Her friend eyed her sideways, hinting at the conversation to come once Miss Woodward had left.

"I'm sorry to interrupt you. Please continue," Laurel said.

"You didn't interrupt. We were just discussing the services." Maya shifted in her seat.

"Oh? I didn't see you there, Miss Woodward."

"Indeed, I wasn't. I was unaware of the services until after they took place. My cousin didn't seem to think it appropriate for a young lady."

Maya snorted and slapped a hand over her face to cover it. "Perhaps not, but I'd rather not be kept out of things."

Miss Woodward nodded. "I quite agree. I don't know where men get these notions that death is unladylike." She smiled at Laurel.

Laurel ground her teeth. How dare this woman make her like her more? She had all the makings of a friend except her family. It was an impossible situation.

Miss Woodward must have sensed the discomfort in the room as she rose to take her leave. "Perhaps the two of you would like to come for tea someday at Tenwich House?"

They both nodded.

Miss Woodward appeared as though she would say more. "Yes, well. It was a pleasure to see both of you. Don't hesitate to call."

When Miss Woodward vacated the room, Maya grumbled, "I have no intention of returning her call."

"Why, Miss Maya Meadows, are you too good for Tenwich House now?"

"Stuff it, Laurel."

"What was that all about?"

Maya shook her head. "I haven't the faintest idea. She could be sincere about wanting a friendship but knowing where she comes from…Anyway, what brings you here?"

"Do I need a reason to call on my best friend?"

Maya eyed her. "Today you do. You should be mourning or sleeping off the day. It must have been difficult finding your mother like that."

Laurel sighed. "It's better than not knowing. What

I don't understand is why anyone would do such a thing? Tenwich stopped burying people at crossroads years ago. It's barbaric though I know my mother would have been buried there, many of these bodies were meant for the churchyard. Who would do such a thing?"

"That isn't what I'm talking about. I know you miss her. This isn't the way mourning is supposed to be. You've been through quite a lot."

"Thank you, but I'd rather things stay normal, or at least as normal as they can be, which brings me to why I'm here."

"I knew you had a reason."

"I ran into Sally Reed." Laurel proceeded to tell her about her encounter with the woman, her conversation with her father, and her meeting with Conner Woodward, leaving nothing out.

"That scoundrel. I had no idea."

"Really? You seem to know all the gossip."

Maya frowned. "Not this time, though I knew Lord Tenwich dismissed maids on account of their motherhood. This brings a new element to it." She paused. "I can't believe it of Mr. Woodward. He seemed so normal."

"You must be joking."

"At least as normal as Tenwich gets. I'm doubly sorry that you had to encounter Miss Woodward here. It wasn't my intention to have her as a guest, but I was curious enough to admit her."

Laurel gave her a reassuring smile. "I'll live."

"It's a shame. I thought Mr. Woodward would be the one for you."

Laurel's heart played in her throat. "Now I know

you're joking."

"My sister is right, you underestimate yourself. He's been after you since we were children."

"Then why did you always tease me about my affections?"

"Don't be daft. I wouldn't have teased you if it was one-sided. I'm not a monster. It's obvious to everyone. Why else would your father warn you away from him? He doesn't want his family joined with the Woodwards after what happened with your mother."

Laurel gave Maya a death stare.

Maya patted her hand. "It doesn't matter now."

"You encouraged me to sleep with him."

Maya viewed her through her lashes. "I thought it would knock some sense into you. Nobody but Lord Tenwich cares if his son marries a commoner, which is odd coming from him."

"What do you mean?"

"Mrs. Margaret Woodward, Conner's mother, was a commoner. She was a merchant's daughter, which is where the family fortune comes from. You didn't think Lord Tenwich made his money through his tenants, did you?"

"I suppose I didn't give it much thought, but how does that give me an advantage? My family doesn't have any money."

"It doesn't matter. Mr. Woodward has all the money he needs. He can marry anyone he wants with his father's blessing." Maya caught her gaze. "He can marry for love."

Laurel's heart somersaulted wildly in her chest.

No, Conner was a horrible man. She wouldn't give him another thought. She came to Maya's hoping her friend would distract her and all she found was a fog that laced over her consciousness.

Her stomach twisted in knots. This new information about the Woodwards didn't matter. She had already made up her mind and nothing would change that. Her happiness was in the balance, and abandoning her morals was not following her heart.

"Lord Tenwich would never approve of me."

Maya gave her a knowing look. "You never know what the old goat would say. It's your father who would need convincing, but who's to say love can't win? There is always Gretna Green."

"I'm not in love."

"I didn't say you were."

"You're impossible. I came here to get my mind off the man, and you hammer him into my mind with a chisel."

Maya threw up her hands. "I'm sorry. It's this visit from Miss Woodward. Can we start again? How are you doing?"

Laurel frowned. "It's no use now. You've ruined it." She chuckled. "I would be fine if my father would get off the business with marriage. In any case, I need to head back. I wasn't supposed to be gone at all and I have a basket full of mending to do."

"Fair enough. Visit me tomorrow morning."

"I'm scheduled to go driving with Mr. Masters tomorrow."

Maya laughed. "You have more to tell me. Come after the drive. Leave nothing out. Nothing."

Laurel collected her gloves and shawl and Maya escorted her to the door. Laurel hugged her friend. Her limbs were heavy, and she yawned. The day's events had left her exhausted, but she trudged home to do her work.

As much as she wanted to crawl back into bed, she had to stay awake for the night's activities. It was a full moon, and the witches would be back in the forest, which meant she could put aside her suspicions at last.

Her mind was full of whys and what-ifs, and the day passed without much effort. Her mending and shroud work progressed as did the hour and it wasn't long before night fell over Tenwich. The days had grown shorter, and Laurel missed much of the daylight hours with her musings.

From what she understood about witches, it was unlikely that they buried the corpses at the crossroads, but what of Mr. Boswell? Perhaps the witches had come across him while they were gathering and panicked. Witchcraft wasn't exactly an accepted practice in England, but then again, few things in Tenwich were normal.

Mr. Boswell was a drunk, but he didn't deserve to die for it. The man only hurt himself, but if he had been involved in reburying the corpses, wouldn't it make sense that his body was buried at the crossroads as well?

Too many questions haunted her as she climbed from her bedroom window and into the stiff wind. If the witches weren't responsible, they at least had more information than what Laurel had, and she meant to question them.

Clouds partially obscured the heavy moon and the resulting shadows seemed to watch her. She had inhaled more of the rosemary and sage concoction but hoped she wouldn't need it. Already every shape was a demon dog or a spirit.

Pull yourself together, Laurel.

As she neared the forest, the moon peered out of its hiding place. The shapes took form and her heart lurched in her chest. The details were etched over the ground and the surrounding forms, leaving Laurel room to catch her breath.

Smoke swam overhead and she followed the trail into the forest. The air was thicker as she grew closer, and her eyes stung as a result. She slowed as the fire became clear as it licked the logs fed to it. Five women stood around the flames, less than she had anticipated after the large gathering the previous time.

Laurel took position behind an old oak. The women were unrecognizable behind their hooded cloaks. They seemed to be waiting for something as they stared into the flames. At last, the woman in the green cloak spoke.

"We thank you, Goddess, for putting our people to rest. Today was a sad day for us all as we mourn our brothers and sisters again."

The woman raised her hands above her head. "Please see that our brother Boswell is put to rest. We ask that you find his killer so that he may find his slumber."

Laurel sighed and then yelped when the figure of Randall Boswell walked toward the witches from the forest. Someone's hand stifled her yelp and her chest tightened. The scent of spice drifted to her nostrils. It could only be one man, Conner.

The witches continued to stare at the flames as though Mr. Boswell wasn't standing among them. They didn't seem to notice Laurel's outburst through the crackling of the fire. Her yelp must have died before it reached them.

She squirmed in Conner's grip but stopped when the witch began again.

"Mr. Boswell, although you may have more business, we ask that you find peace. Your killer is among the living and the living will find you justice."

The ghost watched the witch until he spotted Laurel and Conner behind the tree. He moved toward them. It was as if he knew they could see him, and as he advanced, the witch continued to plead with him to find his peace, though how she knew he wasn't at rest was beyond Laurel.

Conner stiffened against her but didn't release her mouth. When Mr. Boswell was within reach, he stopped and met eyes with Laurel.

"Find him," the ghost said, his breath like a crack in the wind. "Find him."

"Find who?" Conner whispered.

"Find him."

The ghost became transparent, and each particle of the being seemed to float away from the whole until there was nothing left of the spirit. The breeze picked up as though to scatter the ghost through the forest like disturbed dust.

The witch lowered her arms and the women murmured something in a language Laurel couldn't understand. One of the witches poured a bucket of dirt over the fire, and Conner pulled her back into the forest.

Her heart slammed against her chest as he released her mouth and tugged her along down the forest path. He stopped near the crypt, far enough away that the witches wouldn't see them.

Laurel stared at him a moment and watched the moonlight bounce off of his hair. He made an impressive figure in the dark as he did in the light, but he seemed to be made for the shadows that accented his cheekbones and defined his jaw.

Laurel swallowed through her dry mouth. "What are you doing out here?"

He frowned. "The same as you, but you missed the interesting parts."

"What interesting parts?"

He shook his head. "You shouldn't be out here. It's still too dangerous. Did you bring your pistol?"

Her pistol. She had forgotten it. She must have made some noise when Conner sighed.

"You could have been killed." He grasped her shoulders.

"What do you care?"

His eyes searched her face. "What do you mean? Of course, I care."

"You would have abandoned me the way you abandoned those maids. I know how it is with you. How it is with your father."

He made a face as though he had a sour taste in his mouth. "With my father?"

Her heart pulsed in her ears.

"I'm nothing like him." He dropped his hands and shook his head. "Is that what this is all about? My father? The maids? This is what you think of me?"

His jaw hardened and she shrank away from him. "I thought you were different."

"Is it true?"

"This conversation is over." He cut a hand through the air, and she flinched. His lips curled away from his teeth. "Some advice—don't listen to everything people in Tenwich say. I thought you knew better."

Laurel stared after him as he stalked off in the direction of Tenwich House. Her hands wobbled at her sides as she fought the tears that threatened. The hollowness in her chest seemed to beat with every breath, and she wished the world would open up and swallow her.

Chapter 25

Laurel stared after Conner as though he had taken her heart with him. She didn't know what to make of what he said so she perched on a bench near the crypt and waited out the uncomfortable sensation.

It was no use. Conner had worked his way under her skin. She wished she could summon him back, but already he was out of hearing. She needed to know what he had meant, but it was unlikely that Conner cared to explain it to her. At least, not after her accusations.

She didn't know what was true anymore, but the sharp twist in her stomach let her know she had wronged him. She was running out of chances with him. Laurel would be lying to herself if she said she didn't care.

Yet, why should she? He was a part of her past now, a childhood fantasy she had entertained. He was as far out of reach as Rollo when he materialized. She had already sworn him off, so what was the problem?

The more she thought about it, the less certain she became. She needed to get home and sleep. She had agreed to take a drive with Mr. Masters, but how could she go through with it now that she knew she was a fraud?

She found her feet and squinted up at the moon. It was well past three in the morning, and she had few answers to the questions that circled her. She couldn't be sure the witches weren't responsible for Mr. Boswell's death, but she was reassured that it was less likely.

Mr. Boswell's ghost hadn't indicated who had killed him, but he did seem less interested in the witches, which seemed answer enough for Laurel. She would find the killer and without the help of Conner, and where the killer resided, the corpse raider could be found.

The cold seemed to lesson, but she knew better than to believe it. It was at that temperature where the cold couldn't feel any lower even though the air was frozen. She watched her breath chase the sky as she crunched over the hardened leaves.

The hair on the back of her neck stood up and a metallic clang brought her to her knees. Eyes forced shut, she groaned and reached for her head, but before her hand made contact, a force slammed into her skull again.

She blinked, trying to see her attacker, but blood spilled into her eyes.

The object (a bar?) found her ribs, and an explosion of sharp pain curled her in on herself.

A scream ripped from her throat, and yet, all she heard was a gurgle.

Her assailant swung again, hitting her back. It was as though she floated above the world in a crush of pain, barely conscious of the bar falling toward her again and again. Her attacker didn't miss an organ or an appendage as she let go.

At last, the attack stopped, but she was too far removed from the world to come back. She fancied she saw Rollo pawing at her bloodied body. When her mother came to join the canine, she knew she was beyond help.

She faded and the pain seeped out of her. She hadn't seen her killer, but he must have been the same man who had killed Mr. Boswell. It didn't matter anymore. She was free.

Her mother smiled at her but shook her head.

Laurel knitted her brows and stepped toward her, but her mother held up a hand to stop her. The image faded but Rollo remained, licking her corpse's face.

A shout penetrated her fogged bubble, and Conner kneeled beside her. He checked her breathing and called behind him, but his words were garbled.

Somewhere in the distance, a hand stroked her cheek, wiping aside the blood. Arms reached around her and hoisted her to a firm chest, and she drifted.

On the tip of her consciousness, she considered her lack of worry, but the absence of pain made her listless.

Her body jostled and more cries came, but none of them were her own. She only came along for the ride. A whisper worked its way through her daze and warmth flooded through her, igniting the pain.

"You're stronger than this. Don't leave me."

A gasp like an infant's first breath shook her. The surface beneath her accented each throbbing bite into her flesh. She groaned and blinked, seeing the contours of the man she had thought she had scared off.

"You're here." Her voice came out a croak. The gaze of her father and Allie stood behind him, and the bed beneath her was her own, but all she witnessed was the presence of Conner.

Conner let out a long exhale and turned to her

father. "She should rest now."

Allie hushed her and shook her head.

Laurel shot out a hand when Conner faced away, bringing him back to her bedside. Words failed to form on her cracked lips, but he nodded in understanding. She was sorry for her assumptions. Sorry, she had listened to her father's prejudice. Sorry, she hadn't given voice to what was in her heart.

Then the pain took over.

Her eyes blinked out and she let the world fade. Somewhere in the back of her mind, she knew she was lucky to be alive, that Conner had saved her life. He had come back, but why? She let the pain wash away her thoughts just as she lost consciousness.

She couldn't tell dreams from reality. She swam in a fog where voices were muffled in the background and the throbbing of her body went to the tune of her heart. She slept.

Somewhere an argument broke out, and her father raised his voice. A quick word from Allie and the room grew silent again, but the unheard words sent a chill through her that quickened the metallic taste in her mouth.

She groaned and the silence lengthened.

What was left of the fog lifted long enough for her to open her eyes. Her father had left the room, but Allie stood near the foot of the bed while Conner sat next to her. The sight tugged her mind with confusion, and she blinked her eyes again as though she could blink away a dream.

"Welcome back," Allie said. Her sister rubbed a hand over Laurel's leg, and a lance of pain shot through her. She flinched. "Sorry."

Laurel found Conner's worn eyes and gave him a small smile.

He forced a smile back, but the strain halted his smile before it reached his eyes.

The pain resting behind her eyes forced her to close them, and when she opened them again, the sun shone through her window, making her squint against the light. Maya sat where Conner had once occupied, or was that a dream?

She licked her dry lips and Maya handed her off a glass of water.

Laurel nodded her thanks. "How long have I been asleep?"

"Not long. Two days."

"Two days?" Laurel attempted to sit up, but her stomach churned as her head swam. She lifted a hand to her head to steady it.

"It could have been much worse. The doctor was surprised you woke up. We thought you would die. What happened to you?"

"I don't know. Someone attacked me on my way home."

"You shouldn't have been out so late, especially not alone."

"You sound like Mr. Woodward."

Maya folded her arms over her chest. "Someone should. He saved you that night. If it hadn't been for him, you would have bled out. Nobody knew you were there."

It was another mark in Conner's favor, but she needed to be sensible. The man was off-limits, even if he had told her the truth before. The rumors lingered between them. They were serious accusations that left

Laurel only with questions.

An iron grip closed over her chest. She appreciated his actions, but that didn't make everything forgivable.

"That isn't all. He insisted on watching over you until he was sure you would recover. He didn't sleep or eat until your father and Mr. Cross nearly dragged him from your side. He deserves a second chance, Laurel."

She wasn't sure she had given him a first chance. "You know it's impossible."

"Why?" Maya's gaze locked with hers.

"It just is. Our fathers would never approve. The people in Tenwich wouldn't approve."

"Damn the people of Tenwich. I'd say a long way has gone to change your father's feelings, but if the old Lord Tenwich doesn't approve, he can go to hell too."

Laurel choked on a laugh. "So unladylike, Miss Meadows."

"To hell with ladylike." Maya frowned. "Someone has to talk sense into you. The man is a keeper, Laurel. He's more perfect for you than Mr. Masters ever was."

Mr. Masters…she had completely forgotten their drive. "Did anyone explain this to Mr. Masters?"

"Oh, he sent flowers." Maya gestured to a bouquet on her bedside table bearing hothouse roses. "Of course, it was expected of him. Mr. Woodward went above that. Don't you see? He cares for you."

"Please, Maya. I was nearly beaten to death."

"And if you hadn't, Mr. Woodward would never have shown his true self."

"Maya, if you're so enamored with Mr. Woodward, why don't you marry him? Leave me in peace where I can get rid of this damnable headache." Laurel rubbed a hand over her forehead and massaged her temples. The metallic taste in her mouth made her surprised her hands didn't come away with blood. "Can we talk about something else?"

"Like what?"

"Who attacked me?"

Maya studied her. "Nobody knows, but everyone is wary, especially in the graveyard. You would think people would think twice about going out alone at night after Mr. Boswell, but it took you to be attacked for them to be cautious."

"Mr. Boswell is different though. He could have been in a drunken fight."

"True, but you should have learned something from it. Even Tenwich isn't safe for people to roam at odd hours."

"Are you sure you aren't Conner?"

"Oh, I know you care now. It's Conner, is it?"

"Do shut up."

"I mean it though. You shouldn't have been out there. At least not without your pistol. Your father and half of Tenwich is looking for your attacker, but nobody seems to have seen anything. It's as though they disappeared."

"Are you sure Mr. Woodward didn't attack me?"

Maya's eyes widened. "That makes no sense. Why would anyone go through the trouble after trying to kill someone? If it was him, you would be dead."

"I suppose you're right." She wanted to think poorly of Conner because if he had redeemed himself, she would have to come to terms with her feelings for him. Of course, it couldn't be that easy. Love never was.

"Why are you so insistent on his poor character?

What happened to your mother was years ago and it was his father's fault. We don't know that he's responsible for the maids, regardless of what Sally Reed says. I haven't heard anything except the usual rumors of madness, which any fool could see are untrue after spending five minutes with him."

"What about his dismissing the maid? He confessed to that."

"There are plenty of reasons to dismiss maids that have nothing to do with pregnancy. She could have been a thief. Did you care to ask?"

She had meant to, but Conner had ended the conversation. "I'll have to speak with Tawny Lowe. I doubt Mr. Woodward would tell me."

Maya shook her head. "It isn't our business."

"Maya, I need to know the truth."

"The truth? I can tell you that. You're in love with him, but you won't let yourself be. There is nothing wrong with falling for someone that others don't like. It doesn't make you any less. It will make you more."

Laurel squeezed her eyes shut. "This is all too much."

"You're right. I shouldn't have sprung this on you right now, but I just wanted you to know that I'm here for you. Whatever you choose, but don't mess this up." She winked. "I'll let you rest now, but it's my turn to watch you."

Laurel rolled over and every inch of skin resisted. The pain shot a groan from her lips, and she fell back onto her back and stared at the ceiling. How could she rest now with the knowledge of Conner's redemption? She needed to see him, needed to apologize, but first, she needed the truth. Had he dismissed maids after getting them pregnant?

Her heart caught in her throat at the accusation she had sprung on him. He had denied any wrongdoing but had admitted to dismissing the maid. Her only answers rested with Tawny Lowe but questioning the woman wouldn't gain favors with Conner.

It was the doubt that made her hesitate, even though she didn't believe the bad things people said about him—it wasn't enough. She had to be sure he was the man Maya thought he was and not the man her father presumed. Once she knew she could trust him, she would do everything she could to fight for him, even if it meant saying goodbye to her father.

Chapter 26

"I'm worried about her, Nathan."

Laurel came awake at the sound of Allie's voice talking to Mr. Cross. The room was dark except for a single candle that Allie had beside her. The two stood inches from each other, speaking in hushed tones. They hadn't yet noticed she was awake.

She closed her eyes.

"We all are." Mr. Cross's voice was low, almost inaudible.

"She doesn't seem to have any direction and this incident in the graveyard." She sighed. "I don't know what else to do."

"Your mother's death was especially hard on her. I'm sure she will come around."

"That's just it, I'm not sure she will. She went out on her own in the middle of the night, for what? Witches?"

"You know she won't stop until she has answers. She's stubborn."

Laurel peeked at them through slit lids.

Allie shrugged. "I suppose you're right, but she needs to wake up. I don't mean from sleep."

Mr. Cross nodded. "I know what you meant. Remember what you were like at her age? You hadn't settled either."

Mr. Cross wasn't wrong. Allie had been almost as

wild as Laurel, but with frivolous things like the latest fashion and gossip. Laurel had missed that stage and went straight to graveyards and shrouds. She would have laughed if her head wasn't in a vise.

"I thought you said you knew her future." Mr. Cross lowered his chin to angle closer to Allie.

Her sister shook her head. "It doesn't work that way. Everything seems to be happening the way it should, but there are exceptions. My father wasn't supposed to drive Mr. Woodward away. Things changed. Mr. Masters is insisting to see her."

Her brief explanation was the most Laurel had ever heard of Allie's knowing. Her sister never talked about it, just as their mother hadn't. It would interfere, they claimed.

"But she doesn't seem to care for him."

Allie shrugged. "It's up to her. I'm not going to encourage one way or the other, regardless of what I know."

"First, we need to find out who's responsible for attacking her."

"I just want her to get better. You know, she ran a fever last night. We thought that was over."

How long had she been asleep? At least now she knew there were no new developments about her attacker. Her father had scared off Mr. Woodward. So, the man sitting at her bedside had been Conner. She didn't know if that had been a dream or not.

Just as Maya had said, Conner cared for her, but it wasn't enough. They were two different people from two different families. As romantic as Maya sounded, she was lighting a fire where there wasn't any fuel. Their relationship had no foundation, and it would never take off.

"One thing your father was sure of, the weapon used on Mr. Boswell was the same weapon used on Laurel. We're looking for one person."

"And the corpses?" Allie asked. "How could one person rob graves so effectively?"

"He made plenty of mistakes."

"Or she."

"It's doubtful the attacker is female. The newer bodies weighed quite a lot. We don't even know if the same person who attacked Laurel is the one who is robbing the graves."

Allie's voice rose. "It makes sense. Are you saying we may have two criminals roaming around Tenwich? It's hard to believe."

Mr. Cross's voice lowered further, and Laurel strained to hear. "Hush. We still aren't sure the two are from Tenwich."

"But nobody has seen anyone new around."

Mr. Cross nodded. "That's true."

"Oh, this is going in circles. I hope father finds something soon. We need to get back to the way things were. I want out of this dress." Allie gestured to the black gown she wore for their mother. Mourning was something Laurel had been lax about.

"I can help you with that." Mr. Cross tickled Allie and her sister squealed. He clapped a hand over her mouth.

She licked his hand and he wiped it away on his shirt.

"That's disgusting." He beamed. "Do it again."

He leaned in to kiss Allie and Laurel clamped her eyes shut. She wanted to let them know she was awake, but she had grown used to their enlightening conversation. She wouldn't catch any more important bits if they were going to spend their time kissing.

Allie moaned.

"Careful," Mr. Cross whispered.

Laurel groaned, unable to keep the peace any longer. Her eyes flickered open just as Allie and Mr. Cross jumped away from each other. Allie's cheeks were a budding pink shade, and Mr. Cross's cravat was crumpled.

She regarded the couple with a smile. This is what she would want with a husband. Someone who loved her like Mr. Cross loved Allie. Did anything else matter? Her parents hadn't been as affectionate, at least not around Laurel, but now, Laurel was determined to see to her happiness.

Laurel stretched out a hand to her sister, and Allie rushed to take it.

"What have you been up to?"

Allie's blush deepened. "Well, I...I'm watching over you."

She patted her sister's hand. "I'm fine. You don't have to watch me."

"I was worried."

"I'm sure."

Allie took a deep breath and exhaled. "More flowers arrived for you."

Laurel's brow arched. "From?"

"Mr. Woodward. Father sent him away."

The new flowers set on a table near the door were not the type you got from hothouses. They were wild, specifically from the graveyard. She smiled at the yellows and whites and purples in the unnamed bouquet.

"They're lovely."

"I thought you'd appreciate them."

"Put them over here." Laurel indicated the place occupied by Mr. Masters' flowers.

Allie lit up and did as her sister insisted. "They don't smell as nice as roses, but they do have a certain cheer."

"Allie," Laurel said. "Don't let my injuries hurt your happiness. I want the two of you to get married. Forget mourning. Mother wouldn't want you to wait."

"Someone has to take care of you."

"Nonsense." Laurel attempted to sit up but ended up on her back. "I do suppose I need some help, but when I'm better, I expect a wedding."

Allie laughed. "You're awfully commanding for someone in need of a lecture."

"You would lecture your poor injured sister?"

Allie eyed her. "You shouldn't be out there alone. If it wasn't for Mr. Woodward, you would have bled out."

"I've heard this lecture before. It doesn't erase the fact that I was attacked."

"Just promise me you won't do it again."

Laurel blinked. "You know I can't do that."

"Laurel."

"Fine. I won't do it again. Will that appease father?"

Allie gave a mirthless laugh. "Nothing short of locking you in your room would settle him. He's disappointed in you."

"I wouldn't expect otherwise."

"We care for you, Laurel. At least don't get

yourself killed."

"Is father here? I'd like to speak to him."

Allie gave her a measuring look. "He's in the workshop but I can go get him for you. It's almost his turn, anyway."

Mr. Cross offered to go, and he left them alone.

"I'm happy for you, Allie. I didn't see it before, but Mr. Cross is perfect for you."

Allie blushed again. "Thank you. That means a lot. I only wish you would settle down."

"In time." Laurel smiled. "Not too long. I promise."

A moment passed before her father opened the door to her room. The open look of relief on his face made Laurel's smile widen. Allie made herself scarce with Mr. Cross as her father grasped her hand in his.

"I'm so glad you're awake. How are you feeling?"

"I'm fine."

He gave her a questioning look.

Laurel shrugged. "I mean, my head is pounding, but it isn't like it was."

He chuckled. "You were always resilient." He studied her. "I remember a time when you fell from that tree outside your window. Now that must have hurt."

Laurel stilled. Could he know about her sneaking out of her window? Was there another time she had fallen out of the tree that she can't remember?

"Yes, I know," her father said, as though reading her mind. "I know where my children are at all times."

"But you never said anything."

He shook his head. "Would it have made a difference? I can't keep you chained up as much as I'd like to at times. I thought you would at least be sensible enough to take your pistol."

"I forgot it."

He let out a breath. "I know I've been unfair to you. You're an adult now and I can't keep treating you like a child."

"This is not where I thought this conversation would go."

His lips tilted up. "You thought I would yell and scream. If you remember right, I've tried that approach and where did that get me?" He gestured to her form on the bed. "I would rather I know where you are getting into trouble than having you surprise me in the middle of the night."

"I thought you said you always knew where I was?"

"That night would be an exception. I thought putting the bodies to rest would give you closure."

She didn't bother to mention the ghosts or witches. Why cause herself more trouble? "I can't help it. I'm restless."

"Which is why I'll allow you to wander the graveyard once again. This time you don't have to do it in secret."

She studied him a moment and then burst into a smile. "Thank you, father."

He held up a hand. "I would like you to forgo your nighttime activities."

She nodded hurriedly. "I don't have a reason to go at night any longer. It would be needlessly dangerous. Besides, I can see better during the day."

"And if it isn't too much to ask, would you leave that Woodward boy out of it?"

"What about him?"

"I know he saved your life, but I would rather not have his influence on our family."

"What influence? I'm an adult like you said. Allie is too smart to do anything stupid."

His shoulders sagged. "I guess you aren't my little girl anymore." He paused and met her eyes. "Are you sure this is what you want?"

She sighed. "I'm not sure of anything anymore."

"You haven't been given the chance to decide. I won't force Mr. Masters on you, but I can't pretend I don't prefer him to Mr. Woodward. He's a fine man."

"And he's completely different from me. We would be miserable. At least with Mr. Woodward, I can be myself. He did save my life." Maybe she did know what she wanted, or maybe her injuries were making her confused. All she knew was that she needed time to heal and think.

"Don't make any decisions now, but if Mr. Woodward wants to court you, I won't stand in your way. I only wish for you to be happy, and if that means I have to tolerate Lord Tenwich during special occasions, then it's a small sacrifice."

"You mean that?" Her heart beat a tattoo.

"Having your child almost die in front of you is the worst feeling that I never want to repeat. If it means letting you go so, I don't have to experience that again then so be it. Make your life. You're not Allie and I don't expect you to follow the same path as her."

A tear came to her eye, but she blinked it away.

"Besides, Mr. Woodward is not his father, and from what I hear, he doesn't usually spend much time at Tenwich House. The Woodwards have a few estates. I don't think you'll have to live with him," he said.

"You're getting ahead of yourself."

He patted her hand and chuckled. "That I am, but I don't think the boy will have any objections. He's taken with you, and I don't blame him."

She sighed. "I don't know if he will be anymore."

"After saving your life?"

"He did what anyone would do."

"He watched over you until I had to threaten him to leave."

She widened her eyes.

"He comes by every day and tries to visit, but I won't let him. Finally, he left these flowers for you."

"Every day? How long has it been since I was attacked?"

"A bare week, I believe."

She straightened in bed, ignoring the woozy sensation it caused. "I've been in bed long enough."

He steadied her with a hand. "At least let your sister help you." He peered over his shoulder. "Allie."

Her sister opened the bedroom door with a sheepish expression. "How did you know I was there?"

He blinked. "Where else would you be? You're always around when we need you."

The three of them laughed.

Their father steadied Laurel when she stood. "See that you get this one dressed. She's got a husband to catch."

"Not quite, father, but soon. I have some things to take care of first. I don't know if he'll have me just yet." A determined thrill raced through her veins, and she gathered her strength to dress. She took a bright white gown from her trunk and shook it out. There was no more mourning.

Her father watched her. "Any man who doesn't come running isn't worth waiting for. Isn't that right, Allie?"

Allie nodded. "He's already done the running. This time, he's waiting for you."

Chapter 27

With help from Allie, she dressed with care. Her father and sister insisted she send for Maya instead of visiting her and it wasn't long before her friend settled into their parlor across from the injured Laurel, who lay back on the sofa.

Maya sat with her hands in her lap and a muted expression on her face. Her best friend knew everything that went on in Tenwich and Laurel meant to test that. At least, her friend would allow her to get started on her investigation, but Maya was having none of it.

"How are you feeling?" Maya asked.

"Like I was run over by a stray carriage." Laurel frowned. "How do you think I feel?"

"You look awful."

"Thank you for the compliment. I must insist you try my new beauty routine. It's called crème de la bar." Laurel smirked.

Maya shook her head. "Have they found your attacker?"

"No, but that isn't why I called you here. Besides, you would have heard about it if they found him."

"Someone is cross today. I'm happy to see you're out of bed."

"I barely escaped with my life, Maya."

"That doesn't give you permission to snap at me. You should be happy you're sitting here and not dead or in a wheeled chair."

Laurel took a deep breath. "You're right. I'm sorry. It's just this headache."

"You should be in bed."

Laurel ground her teeth. "I want answers."

Maya crossed her arms. "Fine."

"Do you know where Tawny Lowe is?"

Maya sighed and dropped her arms. "I knew this was coming. You want to be sure Conner isn't what everyone expects. He's not his father and you know that."

"Maya."

"You don't want to know the answer, but I'll tell you anyway. Miss Lowe was found a week ago hanging from a beam at the Pig's Ears. She hung herself."

Laurel's skin iced over. "But she was pregnant…"

Maya shook her head. "I don't know. Nobody has said anything about a pregnancy."

"Then that's it then. I can't talk to her. I'll never know."

Maya glared at her. "If you would listen to your foolish heart, you would already have your answer. What reason does Conner have to lie to you? The truth always catches up to you. Always. He's smart enough to know that. He isn't—"

"Like his father. I know."

"What's bothering you?"

Laurel studied her friend as though she could unravel her question. "I don't know. I know what I want, but it isn't that simple. I want confirmation. I want a guarantee that everything will work out. I want true love."

"It doesn't work that way. Everything is uncertain,

even love. You can take comfort in the cards you're dealt, or you can throw in your hand. It can't go both ways."

"You want me to take a leap of faith?"

"I want you to trust yourself."

Laurel slouched back into the sofa and toyed with the fringe on her shawl.

Maya was right. If she couldn't trust Conner to tell the truth or that he was a good person, how was she going to be in a relationship with him? Maybe she didn't deserve him after all.

Her friend reached for her hand. "This is normal. You have to learn to trust someone with your heart."

"How do I get past this?"

"You've known Mr. Woodward your whole life. Has he ever given you any indication he was like his father?"

She lowered her chin as she remembered their actions in the study. "No."

Maya nodded. "And has he been anything but a gentleman toward you?"

A flash of their kiss made her lick her lips. "No."

Maya cleared her throat. "It sounds like you already have your answer."

Laurel did trust Conner with her life. How could that be any different than trusting him with her heart? The more she thought about it the more it made sense. Her chest burst with warmth as she thought of his embrace and heated kisses.

He wasn't perfect like Mr. Masters, but he was more like her than anyone she ever knew. He would make her happy, but was it already too late? Had her father warned him off for good?

She straightened on unsteady legs.

Maya's eyes widened. "Where are you going?"

"I'm going to catch myself a husband." Laurel paused. "One other thing—have they buried Miss Lowe yet?"

"Why do you think you can speak to corpses now?"

Laurel shook her head. "I want to know if someone steals her body. She committed the unforgivable sin in the grave robber's eyes. He will want to bury her at the crossroads."

"Are you sure he's still active?"

"No, but why go to the trouble of almost murdering me and killing Mr. Boswell if you're not serious about your goal?"

"You'd think he would give up. You're a witness."

"Something tells me he's more determined than that."

Maya sighed. "Tawny was buried this morning. He couldn't have had the chance to dig her up, not with the mourners nearby."

"Perfect." Laurel headed for the stairs to snatch her pistol and shawl while Maya stared after her with a blank expression. She steadied herself against the wall as she gritted her teeth through her injuries.

Maya sat where she had left her when she returned. "Laurel, I must insist that you rest. You can't possibly aim with that with a head injury."

"All the same. I have to get there before he does and before dark."

"What about Mr. Woodward?"

"He'll understand. I can catch him afterward."

"Fine, but I'm going with you." Maya stood and

straightened her skirts. "Mind you, it better not be muddy. I just bought these slippers."

Laurel smirked. "Oh, it will be muddy. I don't suppose you have a weapon under all that." Laurel indicated Maya's outfit.

Maya blinked. "Of course not, but I do have this." She gestured to the ebony umbrella resting by the door.

"Good enough."

With a quick word to Allie, Maya and Laurel left side by side to investigate the graveyard. The sky was overcast, threatening rain, and Maya stared up at the sky with a frown. Their only consolation was that the wind hadn't started up, and it was warmer than usual.

Laurel went through her routine as they passed the headstones, but this time with enthusiasm. She didn't know what Maya thought but if her laughter was any indication, she at least had a sense of humor about it, which was more than she could say about most people in Tenwich.

Her excitement was contagious, and after a while, Maya joined in her greetings. It had been too long since Laurel had walked freely in the graveyard, and she wanted to take full advantage of it. Her mind was among the dead when her head spun, and her foot caught on a root not far from the churchyard.

She tumbled to the ground, a lance of pain shooting up her leg as she landed on her knee. Maya attempted to catch her, but the force with which Laurel fell was too hard and swift.

"Are you all right?" Maya's eyes were lined with worry.

"I don't know." Laurel flexed her arms and then her legs and winced at the pain in her left ankle. "I'm going to need help."

Maya shook her head. "I can't carry you. I'll have to find someone who can. Will you be safe?"

Laurel quirked a smile. "I have my pistol."

"Good. I'll be back in no time." Maya set off, her slippers sliding along the path they had just taken.

Laurel prodded her ankle, and she winced when the pain intensified. "I suppose I deserved that." She sighed. "I'm always getting myself into these situations."

The clouds overhead darkened, and Laurel frowned at the sky.

"Don't you betray me too."

She closed her eyes, trying to think of anything that would make this situation better. Laurel shifted her weight to a softer space on the lawn.

"You should have stayed out of this," a voice said from behind her.

Laurel dove just in time to have a cane swing over her head. The Vicar stood over her shoulder, a grim expression on his features. "What are you doing?"

"Stupid child." He pulled his cane back again, ready to swing it at Laurel's head.

She held up an arm to protect herself, but the blow landed on her back. She screeched as the metallic jolt claimed her. An electric bolt-like fire consumed her, and she gritted her teeth against the onslaught. Her fingers defied the discomfort and grasped for her pistol in her reticule.

Laurel fumbled with the strings securing her reticule, and the Reverend went in for another hit.

This time, the blow landed on her head, and the familiar tang hit her tongue. Her mind spun out, and it took everything she had not to fall back onto the grave beside her. She kept her eyes shut as blood streamed down her face.

"I should have killed you the first time."

He nearly had. Why hadn't she stayed at home?

She dug her hand into her reticule and attempted to free the pistol. "Why are you doing this? I don't know anything."

He paused. "It's chits like you who give the parish a bad name. Your mother was no better. It's time for you to join her at the crossroads."

Her hands shook as she freed the pistol, but the blood in her eyes made everything a blur. She only had one shot, and she prayed Maya wouldn't stumble on the Vicar. At least, not alone. She wiped the blood from her face as he rambled on, unaware or unconcerned about her weapon.

"They had no business being buried on sacred ground."

"If you blessed the ground, I have doubts about how sacred it is," she snapped. She raised the pistol.

He chuckled and slapped her weapon away, tossing it to the ground. "Now it's time you learned a lesson." He raised his cane again, and she shielded herself with both of her arms. It was just as before, and no weapon or friend was there to save her.

She cowered inward as the blows landed again and again. The blood was replaced in her eyes, and she could barely make out the silhouette of her attacker when another figure rose behind him.

She gasped, but no words made it past her lips as another blow landed.

A growl rumbled through the graveyard and the

Vicar jumped, dropping his cane.

The demon dog advanced, forcing the Vicar to step away. His eyes were wide as though they would pop from his head, and his lips formed a wide o. The dog didn't hesitate as it stalked its prey. At last, the dog had found its catch.

Laurel fell back on her hands when the rain started to fall.

She closed her eyes as the rain washed her face clean, accompanied by the sound of ripping flesh. Her tears joined the rain and blood, and she huddled into herself like a lost child.

The Vicar's cries died as the sky opened up in a fury downpour and a faint gurgle accented the streaming water. Then he was silent.

A shout rang out over the patter of her heart, and she chanced to open her eyes.

Conner rushed toward her, followed by Maya.

Her friend threw a shawl over her shoulders and backed away as Conner inspected her injuries. He brushed the sopping hair from her face and held her chin in his hands.

"I told you never to do that again," He said, his voice heavy with sadness, although the lecture in his words warranted anger.

"I took my pistol."

"Laurel, the presence of a gun doesn't mean you're safe."

Maya fell behind her and grasped her shoulders. "She's had enough for the day. What happened here?" Maya swept a hand over the scene.

The outline of a body stood bold against the obstructing rain, and blood seemed to pool along the graves. The Vicar was unrecognizable on the lawn. The demon dog had claimed his victim.

"The Vicar attacked me." Laurel's voice was a whisper.

"And you ate him?" Maya's brow rose.

"A demon dog," Conner added. "A big one too."

Laurel couldn't puzzle out why she was able to see the dog without help, but the Vicar hadn't had trouble either. It didn't make sense, but at least the dog hadn't used her as dessert. The Vicar was well on his way to whatever hell he preached against.

"Now we're talking about ghosts and witches again." Maya shook her head. "Demon dogs. If you don't mind, I want to get out of the rain before I catch my death. I suggest the two of you do the same." Now that she knew Laurel was safe, she nodded to Conner and skid away.

Conner stared into her eyes and the gray depths of his seemed to echo the shade of the sky. He put a hand under her legs and around her arms and lifted her to his chest.

A cry pierced the air as she dangled in his arms, but the pain seemed to evaporate as he bundled her against him.

"Never scare me like that again." He raised his voice over the storm. "Are you ready?"

"I'm always ready." She laughed.

He paused, studying her face. "I won't let you go."

He carried her without another word, not elaborating but she got the feeling he meant forever. Her heart swelled, and he spared her a grin.

Laurel found his lips, tasting the salty rain as well as his astonishment. His smile widened as he paused to kiss her back. The frozen rain did nothing to stop the heat that flooded between them. Her blood was on fire and not from her injuries.

He caressed her lips the way he might soothe her pain. Her heart raced, outdistancing their pace, and he nuzzled her while planting slow kisses on her lips.

He pulled away, laughing. "You'll be the death of me, but I would die to keep you." And with that, he brought her home.

Chapter 28

A week passed without a word from Conner. Laurel slept most of the time, not expecting anything different from Mr. Woodward. Her body was bruised from her scalp to her toes, and she refused to look at herself in the mirror.

The weather lashed outside her bedroom window, making the tree dance for her amusement. She wanted more than anything to go outside, to confirm what had happened to her, but she knew when enough was enough, and she stayed in bed until Allie encouraged her to sit in the parlor.

She was lucky her wounds weren't more serious, but it seemed her head had been the main target, and she had gone away with a concussion and bruised body. Everything ached but she refused the laudanum offered her, wondering if it too would produce ghosts.

Allie made jokes about her hard head, but in truth, it was what had kept her alive. She would never know what she had done to provoke the Vicar, but it seemed she wasn't the only one he had attacked.

The doctor confirmed the injuries on Laurel were identical to those found on Mr. Boswell. The demon dog had found its killer. Tawny Lowe's grave had been undisturbed, but a shovel with blood was found in the Vicar's house.

Laurel shared nothing of the witches to the

magistrate, and he never mentioned them. She decided the practitioners should live in peace after their work helping the spirits rest. She hoped that Tawny Lowe was their next target.

This opened up her remaining question; what had happened to the maid? She believed Conner wouldn't abandon his child so that left Lord Tenwich. She could believe nothing else as Mr. Woodward came to call.

He came carrying another bouquet of wildflowers, which were drooping, attesting to the late season. It seemed Conner had been just in time when snow trailed behind him into the house.

Dim light filtered through the parlor window, but nobody dared light a lamp for fear of disturbing Laurel's head. It was enough light to accent the man's high cheekbones and suave black hair as she looked up from the book she attempted to read.

Allie eyed Conner a moment before making herself scarce into the workshop with their father, leaving them alone. Mr. Woodward looked after Allie with tilted lips.

"It has occurred to me that I owe you an explanation."

Laurel made a sound in the back of her throat. "You don't owe me anything."

He bowed his head. "I want to explain."

"What do you have to explain? You're going to be Lord Tenwich someday."

"I'm not so sure about that."

She quirked a brow, but he continued.

"Miss Tawny Lowe was one of our maids. That's true. We dismissed her when she started spreading rumors about my father."

She started to speak, but he raised a hand.

"I believe these rumors were actually true. My father has a history of...well, he has a history with maids. I thought he had changed his ways, but it seems age hasn't made him any wiser." He paused. "When I explained to you that I dismissed her, I didn't realize the extent of your knowledge until your friend Miss Meadows contacted me."

"Maya." Laurel rolled her eyes.

"She came to me yesterday wanting to know why I hadn't visited you." He grinned. "I thought you wouldn't want to see me."

"Why ever not?"

He shook his head. "That's what she said. In truth, I wasn't sure if I was a wanted visitor. I worried I would remind you of your attacks since I was present after both of them."

"You're nothing of the sort."

His grin widened a fraction. "I know that now."

Laurel glanced at the door leading to the workshop. "So, why are you here?"

"I needed to explain what happened with Miss Lowe. Miss Meadows explained to me your hesitations."

"Hesitations?"

He shushed her. "I dismissed Miss Lowe believing the rumors to be false. If it's any consolation, I hear her pregnancy was, in fact, false. It doesn't matter. She was in our employ and my father should never have taken advantage of her. I, however, have never had relations with an employee."

"Why are you explaining this to me?"

"Because, my dear, I intend to marry you."

She stared forward, stunned. "Why?"

"It's come to my attention that if you love someone, you should marry them."

"You love me?"

"I see I've driven you senseless. Yes, I love you. I've loved you since I laid eyes on you as a child. I looked at those fat brown curls bouncing on your head and told myself this girl is the one I was going to marry."

"I'm a cabinetmaker's daughter, Mr. Woodward. It would be a horrible match for you."

He shook his head. "It doesn't matter. I don't care to be a baron any more than you care to be a cabinetmaker. If my father decides to disinherit me, then, by all means, let him. It's you I want. I can find an occupation." He stood from his place across from her and closed the distance between them. "No title or amount of money would keep me from your side. That is, if you will have me?"

"Conner, I've been in love with you my entire life."

"So, Miss Meadows tells me."

"Hang Maya. She's too nosey for her own good." Laurel rose to her feet to join him, and a smile burst from her every pore.

"Then, you'll have me?"

"Of course, I will."

He embraced her, and she fought back her tears. This was real. It was happening, but just in case, she pinched her arm, forgetting her injuries. She jerked back, but Conner held her tighter. Laurel found his lips then and held nothing back.

Their kiss was hurried at first but transformed into a delicate dance between them. She savored the taste of him, coffee and honey, and let her hands travel over his tight arms as he explored her backside.

His tongue savored the taste of her lips, and she reciprocated, exploring the boundaries of their passion. Boundless. A heady warmth formed between them, and nothing would have broken the spell, or at least, nothing but Allie.

"It's about time." Allie spared nothing as she came to hug the couple.

Her father was next to enter. He eyed Conner with a grim frown that twitched into a reluctant smile. "Does he make you happy?"

"Father, any fool can see he does." Allie shook her head.

Laurel couldn't stop smiling. "Yes. A million times."

Conner pulled her away from Allie and her father and found her lips again.

Allie cleared her throat. "There will be plenty of time for that."

Conner and Laurel shared a smile but faced Laurel's family. Yet, he didn't move far from her side, and they would stay that way for as often and as long as they could. They had spent too much time apart, and now, they would make up their time together.

All that was left was for them to face the baron, and as Laurel expected, he wanted nothing to do with her. Yet, he didn't protest their connection either. When Conner led Laurel into Tenwich House, Laurel sensed the stares of the staff as they neared Lord Tenwich's study.

Conner left her in the hallway and let himself into the room, but Laurel could hear them clearly through the door.

"Conner, I'm not interested in your excuses or your whore. Get out of my sight and come back when you've gained your senses."

"If you would give her a chance—"

"She's beneath you, son. You need a woman who can raise the status of the barony not lower it."

"Hang the barony."

Lord Tenwich snorted. "You say that now, but when the time comes that I have passed, you'll think better of it."

"I doubt that."

"Be that as it may, I don't have another son, and your cousin isn't fit for anything higher than a magistrate."

"Amelia's brother is more competent than it seems."

Lord Tenwich scoffed. "I'll be the judge of who is fit for the barony, and I've already chosen you. Now, you need to pick someone suitable as your baroness, and do it before I die."

"I've already found her."

A strangled sound came from the other side of the door. "Be off with you. I don't want to hear any more about Miss Laurel Atwell. Her mother was a whore, and she's followed in her footsteps."

Laurel's blood boiled, and she clenched her fists at her sides. Before she could stop herself, she rushed into the room. "My mother was not a whore."

Lord Tenwich smiled up at her from his desk, his thin lips almost in a snarl. "I see you brought her with you."

"Laurel, stay out of this."

"Why? It concerns me, doesn't it?"

She rolled back her shoulders. "I'll have you know I'm not the woman you think I am."

Lord Tenwich shrugged. "You're not a penniless slut who wants nothing more than to be a baroness?"

She bit her lip. "My financial state is none of your business."

"I care to differ. You want to marry my son, but he needs social connections, not a woman without prospects or a dowry."

"I hardly think—" Conner started.

She placed herself between Conner and the desk. "What of love?"

Lord Tenwich smacked his lips. "Love is a fairytale. Marriage has nothing to do with love."

Conner held up his hands and placed them on her shoulders, turning her to face him. "Wait. Wait. So, you do love me?"

Her expression softened. "Of course, I love you, you fool. Why else would I want to marry a harebrained future baron? I don't care for your fortune. I'm not accustomed to it, and as far as being a baroness is concerned, I'd rather avoid it. It's you I want."

Lord Tenwich chuckled. "You're both mere children."

Conner rounded on his father. "But you see we care for each other? We're a good match, fortune and titles aside."

Lord Tenwich tapped his fingers on his desk and paused. He watched them a moment, taking his fill of their expressions and examining Laurel in the light of the tall window. "You're a beauty, I'll give you that."

"Father, I'm not asking for your permission, but I'd

rather have your approval."

The older man sighed and ran a hand through his graying black hair. "Fine. Marry her, but don't come running back to me when you see you've made a mistake. I know you care nothing for the barony, but you will uphold it, and hopefully, your children will have more sense than you. God rest your mother she was to hear of this."

Conner made a sound in the back of his throat. "Mother would approve."

"Perhaps, but I guess we'll never know. Get out of here before I change my mind."

Laurel's smile showed her teeth as Conner led her from the room. They stopped in the hallway where Conner fell to his knees.

"My love, my angel." Conner kissed the tips of her fingers.

"What are you doing? Get up."

"I wanted to give you this and make you my proper bride." He rustled into his greatcoat and fished out a shining gold ring. An intricate display of diamonds and leaves accented the band. In the center sat a golden heart.

Her hand shook. "It's lovely."

"It was my mothers. It took me weeks to find it."

"Weeks? You've been planning this all this time?"

He smiled. "I'd like to say I was but no. I was planning to wed, but I wasn't sure you would have me."

"That day in the crypt. Tell me you didn't pull this from your mother's body."

He chuckled. "It wasn't in the crypt, though I looked there. I found it in the attic with the rest of my mother's jewelry, which will all be yours after we marry."

"Who said I was going to marry you?" She laughed.

He placed the ring on her finger and kissed her hand. "I do."

Her eyes crinkled. "I do, too."

Epilogue

Conner raced after Laurel, taking the steps two at a time. Tenwich House was filled with laughter from the wedding breakfast, and nobody would miss the bride and groom. If they did, who could blame them?

She made it outside his, no their bedroom door before he caught her. He found her wrist and turned her to face him. Both breathless from the chase, Conner claimed her lips, his hands guiding her chin as he deepened the kiss.

Laurel giggled as he tickled her sides and rose on her tiptoes to take better advantage of his lips. Neither cared if any of the household servants came across them. They had waited long enough for each other.

"You're fast but not fast enough." He chuckled.

"Who's to say I didn't let you catch me?"

He grinned. "Did you?"

She shook her head, laughing. She reached behind her and twisted the doorknob as he sampled the skin along her neck just below her ear. Warmth flooded between her legs, and she pulled him into the room by his neckcloth.

"Demanding, are we?" Conner threw his greatcoat behind him.

"You're wearing too many clothes. Here." She pulled off the neckcloth and started on his waistcoat buttons.

"Madam, I must insist you take this off first." He indicated her gown.

She clicked her tongue. "By all means, have at it."

He grumbled as he scanned the garment, fighting the ornamental buttons and the ruffles. At last, his hands settled on the tiny seed pearl buttons on the back and relieved them with shaky fingers. When he, at last, reached her stays, she yawned.

"We should have had your new lady's maid help."

"That would take all the fun out of it."

He ripped the rest of the silk from her body.

"I quite liked that gown."

He made a sound in the back of his throat. "You only had to wear it once."

"Who's to say I won't kill you and remarry?"

His eyes widened. "And risk the noose?" He shook his head. "Unlikely. Besides, my ghost will haunt you for the rest of your life."

He removed her stays and all that remained was her stockings and chemise, which the latter he deftly threw over her head. His hands went to his own clothes and rid of them in record time while she laid back on the bed, her body an erotic display of flesh.

He climbed over her, his skin brushing against hers. She marveled at the sensation of their bodies coming together at last without the constraints of clothing. He nuzzled her face, kissing her cheeks and chin before finding her lips again.

"I've waited years for this," he breathed.

She smiled, and smoothed a hand over his face, and he leaned into her touch.

"Make love to me," she whispered.

"Shush. Let me enjoy this."

He smoothed his hand down her neck and circled her breasts. They grew tight, her nipples hard. She squirmed and arched into his hands.

He chuckled and placed a nipple in his mouth, lapping and sucking the sensitive peak.

She gasped and drew a hand through his hair while he fondled her other breast. She buried his face in her chest with no reservations in her wanton behavior.

He obliged her and made slow circles around her nipples.

"Conner." She threw her head back.

He sucked on her nipple while his hand roamed lower, finding her center where she was hot and wet. He parted her lips with his fingers and traced the outline until she bucked into his hand. His finger teased the waiting flesh and she whimpered into the pillow.

"Please, Conner."

He pressed a finger inside her, and she lurched forward.

"Oh, God."'

His lips returned to hers, and she panted into him as he stroked her center with his thumb and pleasured her with his fingers.

"I want all of you," she pleaded. She couldn't argue with the hand between her legs as it stroked faster. "Oh God, harder." He plunged into her, and she raised her hips to meet him.

Her hands twisted in the blankets, and she braced for the upcoming storm.

When it hit her, she bucked and shook. A cry tore from her throat.

Laurel melted into the bed, a smile spread across her face.

Conner positioned himself between her legs and teased her with the tip of his cock. She shivered and raised her hips, eagerly awaiting his entrance. He steadied himself over her, and she smiled up at him.

"I'm ready," she said.

"I love you."

He inched closer, slowly entering her and taking pains not to hurt her.

A sharp tug inside her made her whimper, and he paused.

"Want me to stop?"

She shook her head. "It feels better already."

He nodded and plunged deeper, giving her the rest of him. She relaxed around him as he began to thrust. He started slow, watching her face as he made each movement, but grew in pace when she moaned with pleasure.

Her muscles were tight around him, and she pinned him in with her legs. She clutched his shoulders, her nails digging into him. His breaths came in pants as their eyes locked.

She raised her hips to meet his.

"Just like that," he whispered.

His thrusts grew harder, and she bit her lip as a torrent of pleasure washed over her.

"Oh, Conner."

He drew in and out of her in slow, deliberate thrusts. Each time a wave rushed through her, and she neared her climax.

He pumped into her, and each time was wilder than the last. They were a symphony of movement, joined in harmony, and euphoria.

A groan escaped his throat, and she clamped down

on him.

Their voices rose and fell together as she convulsed around him, and he spilled his seed inside her. A dam broke, leaving nothing left of her reservations.

He collapsed on top of her, panting.

She hugged him close, wishing he would never leave.

Laurel pushed an inky lock of hair out of his face. "Do you think they've missed us?"

He chuckled. "They probably heard us from the drawing room."

She covered her eyes. "I'm not going back."

"You never have to." He nudged her with his nose. "Stay with me forever."

Her smile was wide and content. "Forever."

A word about the author...

Mae Thorn enjoys being romanced and terrified- a combination not normally found in books so she writes them. Her favorite stories include kickass women and the men they fall for. She writes historical romance, fantasy, and horror. She has published three historical romance books: Notorious, Dangerous, and Rebellious.

Mae holds a Bachelor's degree in English from the University of Utah and a Master's degree in Library and Information Science from San Jose State University.

She is the co-president of the League of Utah Writers Romance Chapter, and she lives near Salt Lake City, Utah with her cats; Church, Shadow Moon, and Sabrina, and a puppy, Whiskey.

maethorn.com

www.ingramcontent.com/pod-product-compliance
Lightning Source LLC
Chambersburg PA
CBHW052024020726
47501CB00004B/1227